W9-DGL-728

"You want to be a mother *now?*"

Brent sounded shocked and Shadow couldn't help but smile. "Don't look so worried! You're in no danger. I'll probably go through a clinic. You know, artificial insemination and all that."

Brent recovered enough to comment. "That doesn't sound like any fun."

"No, it doesn't. But then, the alternative isn't always that great, either."

Brent quirked a brow at that artless confession, then laughed when Shadow slapped her hand over her mouth.

"Forget I said that," she mumbled past her fingers. "I didn't mean to cast aspersions on the male species and their abilities."

Brent grinned. "I was taking it more as a challenge."

"Well, for Pete's sake, don't! I certainly didn't mean it as one."

"Still," Brent said, "as long as we're both in agreement that marriage isn't what we're looking for, I think we can have some of your acclaimed *fun* together. Don't you?"

"I suppose," she agreed, but without as much enthusiasm as Brent had hoped for.

Dear Reader,

May marks the celebration of Get Caught Reading, a major campaign in North America created by publishers to promote the joy of reading. Why not visit your local bookstore, shop online or go to the library? I hope you're caught reading Lori Foster's latest Temptation novel, *Sex Appeal!*

May also marks the launch of HEAT, an exciting new promotion in Temptation. And who better to lead off this program than Lori, a writer known for her sensuous writing style? In the months to come, watch for more hot, passionate reads from all your favorite Temptation authors.

In September, look for Lori Foster's first Harlequin single title, *Caught in the Act,* followed by two special linked Temptation novels in October and November.

I hope you enjoy all our wonderful books and "get caught reading" today!

Birgit Davis-Todd
Senior Editor & Editorial Coordinator
Harlequin Temptation

Get ready to feel the…

Lori Foster
Sex Appeal

HARLEQUIN®

TORONTO • NEW YORK • LONDON
AMSTERDAM • PARIS • SYDNEY • HAMBURG
STOCKHOLM • ATHENS • TOKYO • MILAN • MADRID
PRAGUE • WARSAW • BUDAPEST • AUCKLAND

If you purchased this book without a cover you should be aware
that this book is stolen property. It was reported as "unsold and
destroyed" to the publisher, and neither the author nor the
publisher has received any payment for this "stripped book."

To RBR, Romance Books and Readers online loop.
There's not a nicer group of fans and friends
to share my morning coffee with.
You give me the perfect way to start each day.
Thank you!

ISBN 0-373-25929-8

SEX APPEAL

Copyright © 2001 by Lori Foster.

All rights reserved. Except for use in any review, the reproduction or
utilization of this work in whole or in part in any form by any electronic,
mechanical or other means, now known or hereafter invented, including
xerography, photocopying and recording, or in any information storage
or retrieval system, is forbidden without the written permission of the
publisher, Harlequin Enterprises Limited, 225 Duncan Mill Road,
Don Mills, Ontario, Canada M3B 3K9.

All characters in this book have no existence outside the imagination of
the author and have no relation whatsoever to anyone bearing the same
name or names. They are not even distantly inspired by any individual
known or unknown to the author, and all incidents are pure invention.

This edition published by arrangement with Harlequin Books S.A.

® and TM are trademarks of the publisher. Trademarks indicated with
® are registered in the United States Patent and Trademark Office, the
Canadian Trade Marks Office and in other countries.

Visit us at www.eHarlequin.com

Printed in U.S.A.

1

YOU'VE BEEN A BAD BOY. *Go to my room.*

Those particular words, boldly printed on a soft, white cotton sweatshirt and drawn tight across a rounded female chest, caught Brent Bramwell's eye. He'd been perusing the new strip of eclectic shops, seeing that everything was in order now that most of the spaces had been leased, when he'd caught the flash of movement in a display window.

Curiosity got the better of him, and despite the icy chill of the early November wind, he slowed his gait. All he could see of the body in the sweatshirt was the middle. Involved in hanging new blinds, the woman stood on a stool or step ladder, her face hidden from view by the sagging blinds. The windowsill concealed her legs from her thighs down.

But what he saw in between—now *that* was enticing. Curvy hips, slim thighs, luscious breasts.

He approached slowly, ignoring the lash of frozen snow pelting his cheeks and tossing his hair. He read the words on the sweatshirt again and wondered what type of female would advertise such a suggestion. Close to the window now, only a few feet away, he stopped to stare as she stretched upward. The sweatshirt rose to give him a view of the smooth, pale skin of her midriff. He even glimpsed her navel, a shallow dent in a very cute belly.

He caught his breath and in that instant she stepped down, looking directly at him. Her huge light-brown eyes, heavily lashed and faintly curious, sparkled with humor.

He fell. *Hard.*

Literally. His feet slid out from under him on the icy walk and Brent found himself flat on his back staring at the gray, blustery sky, the wind temporarily knocked from his lungs.

He was still struggling to breathe when he heard the shop door open. The woman rushed outside, the cold air ruffling her dark curly hair, then she, too, did a slip-slide act as she attempted to maneuver on the ice. Doing a better job than Brent, she caught her balance and knelt beside him. As she reached for his head and cradled it between her warm palms, he stared at her— stared into the prettiest brown eyes he'd ever seen. They were deep and compelling.

Her voice anxious, her cheeks flushed, she asked, "Are you okay?"

Brent searched for something to say, but came up blank. He simply nodded, not sure he could speak. Embarrassment warred with discomfort. The sidewalk was hard, scattered with bits of salt and ice, and so cold his teeth began to chatter.

She frowned. "Let me help you up. Can you walk?"

He started to respond with a disgruntled "yes," then thought better of it. She was cute, not shy in the least, and he was interested. "I think so," he answered, then waited to see what she would do.

Without hesitation she slipped one arm beneath his shoulders and attempted to help lift him. Brent was a big man. Another man would have had a hard time supporting him, but she tried, he'd give her that. He felt her slim arms go around his waist, felt her shoulder wedge into his armpit as she pulled his arm over her shoulders. Her softly curved hips pressed into his thigh. Once they both stood, he towered over her.

Together, slipping around a bit, they started forward. He gave her only a little of his weight, just enough to keep her glued to his side. She led him into her shop. "I'm really sorry about that. They've been throwing salt down all afternoon, but with these temperatures, the ground just keeps freezing." She peeked up at him, mesmerizing him with those big brown eyes. "I hope you didn't hurt anything."

She was, without a doubt, adorable. Her dark, curly hair was cut in a tousled style and looked as fine as silk. Her cheeks were now very pink from the cold, but otherwise she was pale, her skin flawless. Brent leisurely looked her over as she led him to a seat behind the checkout counter.

She had on very snug, faded jeans and white leather sneakers. The sweatshirt was softened by age, adapting to her body, to her breasts. Now that he was sitting down he could examine her more thoroughly. He didn't miss the fact that her nipples were puckered from the cold.

"I'm fine," he told her as she peered at him anxiously. "I believe I only bruised my pride."

Her wide grin took his breath again. "Oh, I don't know. I imagine you may have a few other bruises as well if you take the time to look closely."

Surprised by her brazenness, Brent said, "It's possible, I suppose." Then he asked, "Who are you?"

Thrusting out her small hand, she said, "Shadow Callahan. Proprietor."

Brent took her hand and continued to hold it, noticing how small and delicate it was. And warm, despite the cold. "Shadow? That's an unusual name."

"Yes, well, most everyone tells me I'm an unusual person."

"How so?"

Shadow glanced down at their clasped hands. Her grin widened. "Isn't this a rather long handshake? According to an article I recently read, when a man retains his grasp on your hand for more than three seconds it's an unqualified come-on." Her eyes twinkled at him. "Are you per chance coming on to me?"

Brent was totally taken aback. He released her hand, but he did so slowly, refusing to let her see his surprise. He said deliberately, "I believe I was contemplating exactly how 'bad' I would have to be to get sent to your room."

She disconcerted him again when she laughed. "I didn't expect to see anyone today. The shop is closed for the rest of the evening. Usually I only wear this around close friends."

"Close male friends?"

She shrugged, drawing his eyes to her breasts once again. "A friend is a friend, regardless of their sex."

"Ah. Not true. Men only befriend attractive women when they have ulterior motives in mind."

She crossed her arms and leaned back on the wall, completely at ease. "You speak from experience?"

He openly studied her. "Of course."

"You know," she drawled, still smiling, "you look like the devious type. Let me guess at your name. Hector? Lucius? You look like a Lucius, with a foul and evil mind."

"If that's so," Brent answered slowly, somewhat irritated by her bold manner, "why did you bring me inside? Wouldn't you consider it dangerous to let a large, devious man in when you're all alone?"

She gestured at the uncovered windows and the flow of human traffic on the walk just outside. "I think if anything too outrageous or risqué occurred, someone would surely notice."

He rubbed his chin. "I suppose you're right."

"Don't sound so disappointed, Hector. I really didn't have the time right now to be ravished, anyway."

"Will you continue to call me Hector if I don't introduce myself?"

"Of course. At least, for about two more minutes. Then I'll really have to insist you allow me to get back to my chores."

Brent stood and formally offered his hand. She took it. "You'll be disappointed to know I'm an angelic Brent. Not a Hector. Brent Bramwell to be exact."

With a slight smile, she looked him over from head to toe. "It fits. And you're wrong. I'm not the least disappointed to meet you, Brent. On the contrary, you're just what I've been looking for."

She appeared amused as Brent again held her hand too long. "I must have fallen harder than I thought. What did you say?"

"You heard me right," she assured him as she pulled her hand free. "Just look at you. Tall and handsome. Your coat is a little concealing, but I believe you're even well built. And not too old. About mid-thirties?"

"Thirty-four," he answered automatically, then asked, "What exactly am I being interviewed for?"

SHADOW LAUGHED, drawing up another stool for herself and gesturing for Brent to sit.

He really was very attractive. She'd noted that right off. His green eyes were intent and direct, his tawny brows heavy, now lowered in an annoyed frown. He had lean features, his nose straight and narrow, his cheekbones high, his jaw firm. And his mouth... He had a very sexy mouth, sculpted, his bottom lip slightly full, a small dimple in his left cheek. She sighed.

Best of all, at least to her way of thinking, he had a dry, droll kind of wit that amused her. There were very few things she liked more than laughing. She was finally at a point in her life where she could indulge to her heart's content in the sheer happiness of being alive. Her constant and unwithering optimism was one reason people always thought she was different, perhaps even a touch strange. And even that she found amusing.

Her perusal of his person had him looking ready to spit, so she decided to explain. "The specialty stores in the complex have decided to group together and have a contest—we're calling it 'Love and Laughter.' Each of us is responsible for finding ten men who fit the description of what single women are looking for—mainly attractiveness, a sense of humor and a romantic nature. Photos of the contestants will be on display in our shops, and any woman coming in can vote for her favorite, one vote per visit. Of course, we hope that'll mean more traffic to the stores."

Apparently she'd shocked him again, so she went on before he could collect himself and start objecting. "There's lots of incentive for guys to enter. Each shop is contributing. The grand prize—the contest winner takes a lady of his choosing on a paid vacation—will be supplied through the travel agent. Photography's being supplied by the photographer two doors down. There are other prizes, like free coffee and a Danish every day for a month, and a variety of discount coupons. A two-hundred-dollar gift certificate from me. All in all, it's a pretty impressive package.''

Brent didn't say anything, simply stared at her with narrowed eyes. Shadow had a hunch she'd somehow offended him, or at the very least, irritated him. She asked curiously, ''How tall are you?''

That brought him to his feet. ''I think I'll be going now. It was, uh…uncommon meeting you.''

Shadow scrambled after him, wondering exactly which part of what she'd said had been too much, when he abruptly halted. He gazed around her small shop in something akin to wonder, his eyes alighting here and there on particular items. ''What the hell kind of business is this?''

Immediately affronted, Shadow propped her hands on her hips. ''It's a novelty shop.''

Brent took two long strides toward the door, stuck his head out and looked up at the sign overhead. ''*Sex Appeal*? What kind of a name is that?''

''I'll have you know a friend of mine in advertising came up with that name, along with a nice advertising campaign. She also contributes some of the slogans I use on shirts and things.'' His eyes were so dark now they looked black rather than green. Shadow tilted her head. ''Would you like a brochure?''

He turned to face her. ''Why don't you just explain to me what type of business you're running here.''

She frowned, feeling stubborn for just a moment, then shrugged. It really wasn't worth getting annoyed over. She ran a hand through her hair, glanced around and wondered where to start. ''I sort of specialize in sexy items," she said finally. "Not your usual silk and satin negligees. I'm not that serious and I don't think love should be, either. What I sell is *fun*. And comfortable. Sexy can be fun, and vice versa, if the right woman wears it. I think men have known that for a long time."

She saw that she held his interest, and expounded on her theories. "I took a poll once, and do you know most men thought women looked very sexy when they were rumpled? Can you imagine? I mean, women run around all the time trying to be perfect. Perfectly manicured, perfectly attired, smelling perfect with their hair styled perfectly. It's all nonsense."

He didn't look convinced.

"One man," she said, "who'd been married to his wife for ten years, told me it really turned him on to see her in her apron, cooking. Another told me his wife was sexiest when she first woke in the morning, all warm and drowsy. There was a young college guy who said the sexiest thing he'd ever seen on any woman was a pair of well-worn cutoffs. But a sense of humor was top of their lists."

"So what do you sell?" Brent asked, his curiosity snagged. "Aprons and cutoffs?"

Shadow scoffed at him. "Of course not. I sell shirts, like this one, that are just plain humorous. And underthings made of the softest cotton, which I can tell you is a lot more comfortable than silk." She didn't miss the way his eyes widened, possibly over her disclosure of the type of underwear she preferred. She crossed the room to lift a nightgown from the rack. "Take this gown, for example. It's soft and warm and comfortable." She slipped her hand inside. "But also pretty much transparent. See my fingers?"

He watched as she pressed her palm against the bodice of the gown. "Hmm."

"And all these tiny buttons down the front are a challenge. Can you just imagine standing there, waiting, watching while a woman—"

"You?"

"Any woman you want," she clarified, "undid all those little buttons?"

"She could just pull it off over her head."

Exasperated, Shadow said, "That wouldn't be any fun. You have to use your imagination a little."

"I'll try to keep that in mind."

She stared at him, the gown hanging from her hand. "All right. I can see you aren't the type to appreciate humor at just any old time." She returned the gown to the rack. "Would you still like to fill out an application for the contest? I need three more men to meet my quota."

"I'll have to think about it."

At least he wasn't turning her down outright. She took a little comfort in that. "Don't wait too long," she cautioned him. "We have to have all the entrants photographed before the end of November. The contest will run the first two weeks of December."

"Photographed? As in posed in some lewd and revealing way?"

"Of course not." She almost laughed at his appalled expression. What did he have to hide? she wondered. Hoping to reassure him, she said, "You don't have to expose yourself, but we are encouraging the rugged look. You know, jeans and boots. You can show your chest if you want, but that's all. The friends I talked into entering wore flannel shirts or sweaters. This is a classy operation. No sleazy shots allowed."

Brent pursed his mouth, his darkened gaze going over her once again. It disconcerted Shadow.

"What are you doing?" she asked.

"Thinking."

"Oh? About what?"

"Actually," he said, his smile very nice, "I was thinking we should have dinner and discuss all this in more detail." He looked at her ringless hand pointedly. "You're not spoken for, are you?"

"Only by about a half dozen guys. Nothing serious." Despite herself, Shadow was interested. He was a little aloof, a little uptight, but he was still a hunk and quick with the banter. "What about you?"

"Is that part of the criteria?" he asked. "That I have to be single to enter the contest?"

"No. That's part of the criteria if you want me to have dinner with you."

"Then I suppose I should admit I'm entirely single, new to town and therefore completely alone and unattached."

"All that?" She grinned, realizing that he was flirting with her. She liked it. "Truth is, I'm fairly new to this area, too, although I've already made several friends, so I can't claim to be entirely alone."

He glanced at his watch. "I'm late now for a meeting, but I can come by and pick you up in an hour."

Shadow tilted her head, studying him. "Why don't we hold off on dinner. After all, I don't really know you. Your name could be Hector, and you might have lied about the rest. But I'd be glad to have lunch with you tomorrow. Here? At the coffee shop?"

He hesitated so long, Shadow was afraid her reserve had chased him off, but she had to be cautious. She knew that.

She was ready to call the whole thing off herself, hoping to save face, when he said, "You have beautiful eyes. I've never seen that shade of brown before. Warm, like whiskey. Lunch will be fine. Around noon?"

He'd said it all in one long, drawled comment. Had he done that on purpose, mixing outrageous compliments and suggestions to take her off guard? "Noon would be fine. I'll meet you there."

"No. I'll come here and we'll walk up together." As he left, he picked up one of her brochures, and Shadow saw him make note of her name and business number printed in the upper corner. He left without another word, this time stepping very carefully onto the icy walk.

After he'd gone, Shadow put her hand over her heart. It drummed madly against her palm. Good grief, a man like that carried a lot of impact, and she'd barely gotten to know him. Still, she'd recognized right off that he liked to control all situations. He had been equally put off by, and intrigued with, her bold manner.

Lunch, she thought, should prove interesting.

AFTER A LONG NIGHT of pondering possibilities, Brent had decided he was pleased to be leasing business space to Shadow Callahan. Very pleased. "Micky, I need you to hunt up a file."

"Yes, Mr. Bramwell. Which one?"

Brent lounged back in his office chair, his eyes on the brochure laid open on his desk. "Ms. Shadow Callahan. She's leasing at the new buildings over in Southwatch."

"I'll have it in a minute."

"Thank you." Brent studied the brochure, advertising everything from board games to perfumed oils, specialty clothing to self-help books promising to put the fun back into your sex life. It was so outrageous as to be laughable. And profitable. Brent could easily see such a novel idea catching on. The woman who had come up with the concept most assuredly intrigued him.

He couldn't remember ever meeting anyone so animated, or so lovely. Ms. Callahan, even dressed in old jeans and a sweatshirt, exuded blatant sensuality and confidence. Her appeal had nothing to do with clothing or store-bought fragrances. It was attitude, the way she moved and spoke, the way she smiled so easily. She was sexy as hell.

Brent was always very conscious of women and their motives; he had to be. Women gravitated toward him because of his bankbook and his connections, not his looks, certainly not his character. He could have been a troll with the nastiest disposition and still women would try for his attention. It'd been a long time since he'd felt the thrill of the chase. Hell, it had been a long time since there'd been any need for a chase.

But Shadow Callahan, with all her compliments and open appreciation, didn't know he had money. So why had she been so intent on controlling the situation? He'd recognized that intention immediately, because it was usually his objective, as well. And for a minute or two there he'd actually allowed her the upper hand, merely out of surprise.

Micky brought in the requested folder and Brent got down to business. He'd be seeing her again in just a few short hours, and he wanted to be prepared this time. Shadow—*what a name*—didn't yet know that he held her lease, and that was just fine by him. He'd take all the advantages he could get. But before he had any more verbal skirmishes with her, he'd find out all he could about her, and there was no way he'd let her take him by surprise again.

SHADOW DIDN'T GIVE BRENT a single thought that morning. She was far too busy with holiday shoppers who used her novel stock of items to take care of those hard-to-buy-for people on their lists. She enjoyed it— the rush, the interaction with customers, the excitement over a particular item that someone decided was "just perfect!" She didn't have time to waste thinking of Brent.

Yesterday evening, though, she'd thought of him plenty. He was interesting. More so than the men she'd met of late, who mostly bored her with their attentions. She wasn't certain what exactly appealed to her about Brent, but she'd figure it out. When she had the time.

He came in at quarter to twelve, his lean cheeks ruddy from the cold. Shadow sent him a quick smile, then turned back to the young women who were trying to decide between two different board games.

"This one's a little more expensive and it takes longer to play. But the concessions each player has to give were designed and written up by a well-known psychologist, and—" she bobbed her eyebrows "—guaranteed effective."

The women giggled, suitably impressed. Shadow went on, motioning to the other game. "This one's more good-natured fun. You make up your own concessions or rewards as you go along, depending on your partner." The choice was made and Shadow rang up the sale, wishing the women luck and reminding them to enjoy themselves.

Brent approached her, taking in her outfit with careful consideration. Shadow grinned at him. "Do you like it?"

She'd dressed like a snow bunny. Her thick cotton top fell to the middle of her thighs and she wore leggings tucked into soft leather boots. As she turned for him, holding her arms out to the side, Brent read the words written across her back: *Face It—Forty Never Looked This GOOD.*

He shook his head. "Very nice. But you're not forty."

"How would you know?" She was thirty-one, but she hadn't told him that. She smiled. "My driver's license is safely tucked away in my bag. Have you been peeking?"

All he said was, "I know you're not forty."

"Do you think I look good for forty?"

"Too good," he said meaningfully. "I thought women always claimed to be younger, not older."

"Now why would I do that? If I said I was twenty, people would think I looked terrible for such a young age. But for forty, I ain't so bad."

"Lady, I think you look damn fine regardless of your age."

He said it so sincerely her heart gave a quick thump of excitement. She hid that reaction well. "Let me get my coat, drag my assistant up from the back and then we can go."

When Shadow returned from the back room, she was followed by a woman whose arms were ladened with printed bedsheets. As Shadow shrugged into her coat, she made introductions. "This is Kallie, my indispensable right hand and a very nice, if somewhat shy, lady. Kallie, this is Brent Bramwell. We'll be down at the coffee shop if you need me."

Kallie smiled. "Take your time. I can handle things."

"Of course you can. I never doubted it for a minute. When you finish stacking those, hang one up so everyone can see the print, okay? Maybe even near the window, where passersby will catch a glimpse of it."

Brent took her arm and led her out the door. "What do the sheets have printed on them that you want everyone to see?"

Even with their heavy coats and the frigid wind, Shadow could feel the warmth of Brent beside her. She dodged an icy patch and stepped closer still. "The, ah, proper placement of body parts."

Brent missed a beat, then laughed. "You're kidding."

"Nope." She crossed her heart. "It's kind of a visual instruction manual. I expect them to be big sellers."

"Have you bought any for yourself yet?"

The coffee shop was only two doors down, so they had already reached it before Brent asked his question. Shadow went in, breathing deeply of the wonderful aroma of fresh baked bread, pastries and flavored coffees. "I love it in here," she said, in lieu of giving him an answer. "There's nothing quite like the smell of yeast and warm bread to make you feel comforted."

"Oh, I don't know. I can think of a few scents I prefer."

Shadow slipped off her coat, took a seat at a small table, then waited until Brent had removed his own coat and taken the seat across from her. Propping her cheek against her fist on the table, she studied him. "I've annoyed you. That's why you're being so outrageous."

Brent cocked one eyebrow upward. "Outrageous? I thought I was making idle conversation."

Shadow watched him a moment longer, then sighed. "Okay. No, and I suppose that's true for many men, and probably many women as well."

"I beg your pardon?"

She laughed at his confusion. "I was answering your questions, since you claim they weren't outrageous. No, I don't own a set of the sheets, and I agree many men might name scents other than baking bread as appealing. But that's also true for women."

"But not you?"

She wagged her finger at him. "Me, I like baked bread. Very safe, you know. Ah, here's Eliza."

Shadow went through more introductions. Eliza, one of her friends, looked Brent over with a calculating eye.

"I'll have a salad," Shadow said, interrupting the intent scrutiny, "and a tuna sandwich on rye, with an apple tart for dessert."

Brent glanced at the menu briefly, then ordered the same.

"Do you want to try today's special coffee blend?"

Before Brent could answer, Shadow said, "Sure. Bring us a pot."

As Eliza walked away, Brent frowned. "What exactly is the day's special blend?"

"I have no idea. But her coffee is always wonderful. And I like to be adventurous." She stared at her water glass and added, "Don't you?"

Brent leaned back in his chair. His eyes glittered with intent, giving her just a shade of warning.

"I'll be busy most of this week getting settled in," he

told her, "but if you're really so adventurous, why don't you agree to have dinner with me on Friday?"

It was only Monday. Shadow felt a little crestfallen that he didn't want to see her again until the end of the week. "I don't know. I'm not at all sure you're trustworthy. Gorgeous, but also a quick talker. I get the feeling you can be dangerous, and I'm usually pretty good at reading people. I didn't used to be...." She shrugged. "But I am now."

"You sound cautious, not adventurous."

"There's a difference between being adventurous and being just plain stupid." Leaning forward in her chair, she stared at him and said, "I am never stupid."

She saw his mouth quirk the tiniest bit at her indignation, but his reply was mild enough. "You don't need to convince me. I've been going over your brochure. It's obvious you're an intelligent woman with a head for business."

He sounded as though he meant that, but Shadow wasn't sure. She didn't want to be drawn in too quickly. It was enough that she found him so attractive, so charming. To be complimentary and observant, too, would almost make him a saint, and she wasn't fool enough to believe that.

Eliza brought their food, and they both were quiet until she'd finished serving them. Their eyes met several times, but it wasn't until after Shadow filled her mouth with a large bite of salad that Brent asked, "So. If you don't want to go to dinner, what would you like to do? I'm settling into a new house this week, but I'm sure I could organize well enough to have you over if you just want to skip the preliminaries."

Shadow chewed thoughtfully, not hurrying, aware

that Brent baited her for some reason, that he felt justified in being so scandalously blunt.

Dressed in a dark gray business suit with a finely striped shirt and silk tie, he was the epitome of male elegance. A very expensive diamond watch peeked out from under the cuff of his shirt, and his hands were large, with light brown hair sprinkled over his knuckles. Shadow picked up her napkin and dabbed at her mouth. She'd given herself plenty of time to think.

"What do you do for a living, Brent?"

His eyes narrowed slightly. "I'm in real estate. Now why don't you answer my question?"

She twirled the spoon in her rich, dark coffee. "You're wealthy?"

Brent sighed, leaned back in his chair and crossed his arms. "Your train of thought is a little hard to follow. Or do you need to know how much money I make before you'll tell me exactly what you want from me?"

Shadow felt bone-deep regret, she really did. He had seemed so different from other men. She stood, opened her purse and dug out a few bills to cover the cost of her meal. She could feel Brent's silent attention, but it wasn't until she'd slipped on her coat that she said to him, "I don't want anything from you. Unless, that is, you want to fill out a contest entry form. I still need three more men for that." She pulled her purse strap over her shoulder and smiled down at him. "Thanks for sharing lunch with me. It's been...educational."

Disbelief crossed his features. She turned and headed for the door without a backward glance. A stunned silence hung behind her for only an instant, then she heard the sounds of Brent scrambling to his feet. She had almost made it to the entrance of her shop when he caught up with her.

His large hand encircled her upper arm, pulling her to a halt and turning her to face him. "Wait a minute."

"Have you decided to enter the contest?" She kept her smile polite.

"Forget the damn contest. I thought we were going to have lunch."

Her smile almost slipped. "That was before you made it so clear why you had asked me in the first place. If I'd known what you wanted up front, I would never have agreed to go."

The wind whipped Shadow's hair into her face and made her shiver. She lowered her head against the sting of the cold.

With a sound of disgust, Brent said, "Come on. It's too damn cold to talk out here."

The shop was warm and only mildly busy. Kallie looked up as they entered, then called to Shadow, "You have a delivery in the back."

"Thanks." She turned to Brent. "I don't think there's anything for us to say. It's a pity, really, because you seemed so amusing. But I'm not interested in a one night stand." Her smile now hurt, but she kept it firmly in place, refusing to give him even an ounce of satisfaction. "Thanks anyway."

Brent rolled his eyes. "Oh, no you don't. Not this time. You may not have anything to say, but I do."

Two people looked up, their attention drawn by Brent's harassed tone. With resignation Shadow said, "Come on, we can talk in my office. But only for a minute." She frowned at him over her shoulder. "I have work to do."

Brent was irritated. If his stomping footsteps didn't get that across, his frown was very expressive. Shadow opened the door to the small office and flipped on a light switch as she entered. A large bouquet of yellow roses sat in the middle of her desk. She stopped in midstride, momentarily nonplussed.

Brent nearly plowed into her. "What...?"

Shadow marveled aloud, "Someone sent me flowers!" Picking up the card, she read quickly, then looked at Brent suspiciously. "Did you do this?"

He glanced at the card in her hands. "What would make you think that? Who signed the card?"

"No one. It says they're from a secret admirer."

"Well, since I'm here, and I've made my intentions well known, there's not much of a secret to it, is there?" He sounded more annoyed by the second.

"But then who? The only men I know are friends."

"I told you—"

"Yeah, I know. Men have ulterior motives." She made a face at him. "I should have remembered that when I agreed to have lunch with you."

Brent all but growled. "Why did you think I wanted to get to know you? So we could be pals?" His voice dropped and he took a step closer. "You're a beautiful woman, Shadow. Maybe a little nutty, but I can handle that. And you're the one who started telling me how attractive you thought I was."

"Well, you are." She refused to back up from him, and instead faced him squarely. "A woman would have to be blind not to notice that. But that doesn't automatically mean I want to jump into bed with you. I do have some scruples and discretion, you know."

He seemed to consider her words, then explained gently, "You come across as something of a tease, Shadow." He caught her shoulder, holding her still. "No, don't get mad. If I've read you wrong, I'm sorry. But you can't blame me entirely for getting my signals crossed. It's not often I run across a woman who's as open and outspoken in her conversation."

Shadow stepped away from him, breaking contact. "I've been told before that I should censor my thoughts before I voice them. I try, but sometimes it's just too annoying, having to pick myself apart before I can say what I think."

His severe expression softened. "So you're attracted to me?"

"Yes, of course."

That got her a smile. "And you wouldn't mind getting to know me better?"

"I'd like to. But not if you're only biding your time until you can score."

"Oh, I think being with you would be interesting," he said with a crooked smile, "no matter what the outcome."

There was that disarming sincerity again. "Thank you."

"You're very welcome." He looked relieved, and determined. "So how about we try lunch again? Say, Wednesday?"

She knew she should refuse, but instead she asked, "Will you enter the contest? I still need you."

It was his expression that made her realize how her words had sounded. She *needed* him. He looked at her mouth as he asked, "How about if I let you know on Wednesday?"

It was like being kissed, the way he looked at her. Her heart pumped hard; her lungs constricted. There was no way she could refuse.

Shadow stuck out her hand. "It's a deal."

His palm was hot, his grip strong, and he carefully tugged her forward. Shadow froze as he bent down, but she didn't pull away. His lips were warm, firm, brushing over her cheek in the lightest of touches. She was as stunned by her reaction to that simple kiss as she was by his audacity.

Unwilling to give him the upper hand, even for a moment, she said, "That was nice." She drew a deep breath to steady her voice. "Maybe on Wednesday you can improve upon it just a bit."

Brent laughed. "I'll see what I can do. In the meantime..." He opened his coat to reach inside his pocket. Extracting a business card, he handed it to her, instructing, "If you change your mind about dinner, give me a call at the office. I'm usually there late."

He whistled as he left, and Shadow wondered if she'd eventually figure him out. One thing was certain, getting to know him would be fun, and wasn't that her business? Fun? It had been awhile—a long while— since she'd reacted to a man like this. But she had a feeling it had been just as long since Brent had enjoyed any real fun. She had a feeling they were both in for some surprises.

enough knowledge to understand why people couldn't be more accepting, more open to change. Unfortunately, the more she learned, the more she could be...

2

THE BITTER COLD was refreshing. Originally from California, Shadow didn't think she would ever be bored with Ohio weather. It changed with each month, and she relished waking every day to something other than continual sunshine. Not that it was cloudy today. She had to squint to tolerate the almost magical reflection of sunlight off snow and ice.

The wind whistled down the little sidewalk in front of her shop, whipping the scarf around her neck and nearly dislodging the colorful red bow in her hair. She supposed a dress hadn't been the best thing to wear while hanging Christmas lights, but she rarely planned her days completely. Usually, she just did what she felt like doing, when she felt like doing it.

Today she felt like being outdoors, decorating. And she felt like seeing Brent Bramwell.

She'd thought of him often the past few days. She knew she had him confused, but he didn't seem to mind overly. He had made that crack about her being a little nutty, but she was used to that. Everyone thought her nutty. She liked to think it was part of her charm.

Even throughout her school years she'd been different, always occupied with gaining independence and maturity so she wouldn't have to conform to anyone else's rules. Other girls had been interested in clothes and boys and music. She'd wanted only to garner enough knowledge to understand why people couldn't be more accepting, more open to change. Unfortunately, the more she learned the more she understood just how different she was, and how rigid society could be when faced with the different and unique. She'd also learned to accept what she didn't care to change.

The wind gave a particularly vicious swipe at her skirt, blowing it up and over the hem of her coat. Shadow squealed, frantically trying to push it back down and nearly toppling from her stepladder in the process. It was sheer bad luck, or maybe good, depending on your point of view, that Brent happened along just then.

BRENT COULDN'T BELIEVE his eyes when he saw Shadow balanced precariously atop a rickety stepladder on the slick walkway, her skirt billowing upward to give him an unhindered view of her nicely rounded backside in a pair of red tights. Her arms were stretched high over her head as she struggled to attach twinkle lights to the framing. When he saw her begin to flounder, tangling herself in the lights, he bolted forward.

However, the icy pavement wasn't accommodating to heroism, and he reached Shadow just in time to lose his footing, thereby knocking her from her perch. They both went down, Brent on the bottom, Shadow landing in a sitting position on his stomach.

Stunned, she twisted around to stare at him. His eyes were closed, but they opened immediately to peer up at her.

"Are you all right?" she asked breathlessly.

"This is becoming a habit." The lights she held were now draped over his chest, and her bow had slid forward to hang over one eye. Brent laughed, which wasn't easy, considering Shadow sat on his diaphragm. She bounced slightly with his movements. "I think I would be better if you could remove yourself."

"Oh." She flushed, then quickly scrambled to her feet. It was an ignominious process and Brent, gaining several glances of her slim legs and lush backside in the tights, realized her bottom half was as enticing as her top half. Perhaps more so. He levered himself up to a sitting position, then came slowly to his feet. The seat of his pants was wet from the snow, and when he felt his head, he discovered a bump.

Shadow still wore a pretty blush, but she brazened it out, untangling the lights from her arms and leaving them draped over the stepladder. "Come on inside to my office and let me look at your head."

Déjà vu, Brent thought as she literally dragged him inside. "My head is fine, it's just my pants that are a mess."

Shadow peered around behind him. Luckily, he hadn't worn a suit today, opting instead for casual corduroy slacks, a thick fisherman sweater and a bomber jacket. She looked at his butt, made a tsking sound and hurried him through the door.

Kallie glanced up as they came in, called a friendly hello to Brent, then went back to her work. There were a couple of customers loitering, but they didn't seem to have noticed the comedy on the front walk. He supposed that was something to be grateful for.

Inside her office, Shadow closed the door and turned to Brent. She bit her lip, looked him over, then blurted, "You could maybe take them off and I could try to clean them."

Brent smiled. "First, thank me for not feeling compelled to make any sexual comments in response to your offer."

"Thank you."

He nodded. "The pants will dry. Don't worry about it. Did you hurt yourself?"

"No. You broke my fall." She cleared her throat. "Thanks again."

"What exactly were you doing out there, anyway? You should have a handyman do that sort of thing for you."

"I can take care of anything that needs to be done. I'm not helpless. Besides, I was enjoying myself. Well, at least before my skirt blew up. I, ah, don't suppose you missed that?"

He didn't bother to temper his grin. "No."

Flushing a bit more, she said, "At least my tights covered me completely." She began removing the bow that now hung around her neck, then riffled her fingers through her short curls, pushing them off her forehead. They sprang right back. "Won't you be uncomfortable eating lunch with a wet seat?"

"Maybe we could just have lunch here. That way no one would stare and wonder."

"Women would look regardless, you know."

"Thank you." Damn, she had him grinning a lot. "If we eat here, I can go home and change afterward. I'm not needed in the office today. I got everything cleared out of the way in the hope you could take some extra time off. I'd like to talk a little more."

Shadow looked thoughtful, swinging the bow from her fingers. "I suppose I could. Wednesday isn't one of our busier days. Kallie could probably handle everything. And I would like to spend more time with you."

She never ceased to amaze him. "Are you this open with every man you meet?"

"Why? Does it bother you?"

"No. It's just that I'm not used to women being so blunt. That is, unless they want…"

"What?"

He shook his head. "Never mind."

She waited a moment more, then shrugged. "I never was any good at being diffident."

Feigning disbelief, he said, "I don't believe that."

She returned his smile. "It's just the way I am, and I stopped trying to change myself long ago. But I like you, so I hope you're not so offended you won't want to see me again."

"It'll take some getting used to, but I'll manage." *What a fabrication,* he thought. Get used to her? She fascinated him. "Now, about lunch? Can we order something in?"

She accepted his change of topic with a smile. "I'll run down to Take a Break. Eliza will fix us up something. Do you have anything particular in mind?"

"Whatever you're getting is fine." Brent reached in his pocket to pull out his wallet. Shadow grabbed his hand.

"It'll be my treat." He started to object, and she added with a frown, "I insist."

Brent paused, then went for a compromise. "All right. But only if you agree to let me buy you dinner. Tonight."

"I still don't know you that well—"

"You can pick the restaurant. Surely there must be someplace local where you'd feel comfortable."

She frowned in thought for so long, he said, "I didn't ask you to solve the question of world peace, Shadow."

She finally nodded. "All right."

"Such a concession," he teased, noting her wariness. "What time do you get off tonight? I'll pick you up."

"No. I'll meet you at Reba's in the mall. About seven?"

"I have a feeling that knowing you will be a constant tug-of-war over control." He touched her cheek, felt how soft and warm she was, and shook his head. "If I say one thing are you always going to say another?"

Shadow stilled, her bow dangling from her fingertips. "I wasn't aware," she said slowly, "that you were angling for control."

Careful, Brent warned himself. She was brazen, but she was also noticeably skittish. "Right now," he said with a smile, "all I'm angling for is lunch."

She looked at him hard and evidently came to a few favorable conclusions. With a jaunty salute, she said, "Have a seat. I'll be right back."

Rather than sit, Brent wandered around her office after she'd gone. It was small, no more than ten feet square, with a large desk, two extra chairs and a filing cabinet. She had a window and door that opened to the back alley, and on the sill were several small planters. His business card rested in the center of her desk. There was also a greeting card of sorts, and without any guilt, Brent picked it up to investigate.

It was from her secret admirer.

That amused him, thinking it was probably some young, inexperienced kid hoping to gain her favor. The words inside, written in a bold, masculine scrawl, were brief, stating only that she was basically "wonderful" and that her young swain was "deeply affectionate."

Brent wondered if Shadow was as open with all men as she'd been with him. He didn't like to think so, but that would explain some young pup thinking himself in love with her. She was the type of woman to turn any man's head, but especially someone inexperienced and vulnerable.

Brent was sitting in one of the chairs, his coat beneath him to protect the seat's floral fabric, when Shadow returned. She had a pot of coffee, two mugs and a large white sack of foodstuffs. Brent sniffed, then smiled appreciatively. "It smells good, whatever it is."

"Ham and cheese stuffed croissants with pasta salad. I'm not certain what flavor the coffee is, but we'll find out soon enough."

Shadow served up all the food, poured Brent some coffee, then settled back in her own chair. He had only enough time for three bites before she pulled out an entry form for the contest. "We can fill this out while you eat."

Brent eyed the form with distaste. "I don't know, Shadow. I'm not much for contests."

"Nonsense. You know you're attractive, and you don't strike me as being particularly shy. I still need three more men, and quite frankly, I'm getting tired of soliciting them on my own."

He froze in midchew.

"Ah, I didn't mean that quite the way it sounded."

Brent took a gulp of coffee. It was, unbelievably, flavored with orange and some spice that burned his tongue. "Do you mean to tell me," he asked with incredulity, "that you *have* approached other men just as you did me?"

"Well, maybe not exactly the same." She winced a little. "You're the only man who was alone. Here, I'll show you." She opened a desk drawer and pulled out a file. Within seconds, she had seven photographs, con-test entries attached, spread out on the desk.

Brent was curious, no doubt about that. He leaned forward to survey each picture.

"This is Guy Donovan," she said. "His wife, Annie, made him enter."

"Couldn't he have at least combed his hair?"

"Annie likes his hair that way." Shadow slid another photo toward him. "This is her brother Daniel."

"He looks serious."

"Oh, he is. He's a doctor. His wife, Lace, tried to get him to show his chest for the photo, but he can be stub-born."

"Who's this guy?" Brent asked, none too pleased with the photo of a dark man wearing a devil's smile.

Shadow laughed. "That's Max. He's a rascal, and he was all for taking off his shirt, but his wife, Maddie, re-fused. She threatened to get her own picture taken—the same way—if he dared do that. He's Annie's brother, too."

"You know these people well?" It seemed to Brent she was overly familiar with other women's husbands.

"I met them through Bea. She's the lady who creates a lot of the slogans for the clothes for me. When I was new here, Bea brought them all in to meet me. Now we're friends."

A bit relieved, Brent asked, "Was your secret ad-mirer one of the men who entered, do you think?"

"Actually, I was wondering about that." She turned the remaining photos around. "The young man here is Chad Moreland. He's a pharmacist close by. Friendly but shy. These two older gentlemen are brothers, Dean and Frank Stiles. They own a vet clinic on the next block and they're so funny they make my sides ache.

And this stud," she added, laughing, "is Ricardo. He does the landscaping for the strip mall. He's an outrageous flirt, too."

"Do you think he'd send you gifts?"

"Ricardo? Naw, he's right there in your face with his compliments."

Brent felt a slow simmer of annoyance. "You're saying he comes on to you?"

She lifted one shoulder. "He comes on to everyone female. Young and old. It's just his way."

Brent didn't like hearing that, even though it was really none of his business. "What about the others?"

"They're all just nice guys as far as I know. I can't see any of them doing this." She indicated the card on her desk. "Not only did I receive a card and candy, but for the last two nights I've gotten breather phone calls. You know the type—you say 'hello' and no one answers. I hate that. Though I know it's nothing, just a prank, it still makes me nervous."

Which proved she was no dummy, as far as Brent was concerned. "Maybe you should have your home number changed."

Shadow flushed, picking at the remaining bite of her croissant. "I thought about it," she admitted. "But I had hoped you might call me, and if I had my number changed, there was no way for you to look me up in the book."

Brent leaned back in his chair, still appalled by how easily she shared her private thoughts. It was downright distracting and he had to wonder if this wasn't just another well thought up female game. When elusiveness didn't work, bring out the blatant truth. "I gave you my card," he pointed out. "You didn't call me, either."

She groused at him defensively. "You already thought I was easy! I know the rules, even if I don't always follow them. Women don't call men."

"I wouldn't have minded." He kept his tone gentle, his gaze glued to hers. He reached across the desk and caught her hand. "What did you want to talk to me about?"

"I don't know." She went strangely breathless when he touched her. "I feel...nice, around you. Very aware and alive. I like that. I kept thinking of you, and I just wanted to hear your voice. Don't get me wrong," she added when he frowned again. "I'm not husband hunting or trying to claim love at first sight. It's just that I haven't met a man I was really attracted to in a long time, and it has nothing to do with how handsome you are. It's more that you're different, just as I am." Then she groaned. "Oh boy, now I sound insulting. I mean, I know most people think I'm kind of weird. I wasn't suggesting you're weird, also."

"Shadow." Brent reached one long arm across the desk, gently laying his fingers over her soft lips, silencing her. "I don't think you're weird. Different, certainly, but in a refreshing way. I like you, too, all right?"

Since his fingers were still on her mouth, Shadow could only nod.

"Good. Now, why don't you call and have your number changed, then let me know what it is." He leaned away from her to pick up a pencil from her desk, then pulled a small piece of paper from his pocket. "My home phone number," he said, showing her the paper. "I've only just settled into the house, and the number is still new to me. I can't remember it myself yet."

After copying it down for Shadow, he handed it to her. She glanced at it and said, "You have the same exchange as me. Where did you move to?"

"Woodbine Haven. Are you familiar with it?" Brent already knew the answer to that. He was, in fact, only a few blocks from where Shadow lived. He'd been pleased when he read her file and realized how close they would be. He waited for her reaction.

She disappointed him when she said only, "I know where it is." For another moment she was silent, then, sounding disgruntled, she said, "You really are rich, aren't you?"

What could he tell her? Woodbine Haven was a section of older, grand houses renovated and advertised as a prestigious neighborhood. It was a private section, containing only about twenty houses, and each was huge, with much of the original architecture from over a century ago. Seeing Shadow's disappointment and not really understanding it, he asked, "Is that a problem?"

"No. Not really." Her soft lips twisted in a wry grimace. "But I've known wealthy men and they tend to assume women will do anything they want just because they have money. They're arrogant and condescending and egotistical."

"Probably," he said, his back going stiff with memories, "because most women *will* do anything for money. I can tell you firsthand how attractive women find the size of my wallet."

Her eyes twinkled with mischief. "Don't you have any other sizable assets that could distract them, instead?"

Exasperation crowded out the more unpleasant emotions. "Shadow..."

Laughing, she raised her hands. "I meant your new home, of course! Woodbine Haven is positively extravagant!"

Brent shook his head in mock reproach. "As soon as I can manage it," he warned softly, "you're going to view the rest of my assets, firsthand."

She attempted to hide her grin and failed miserably. "Well, in the meantime, how about filling out the entry form? *Please*."

With a dramatic sigh, Brent agreed. "If you insist."

Shadow stood to clear away the remains of their lunch, and it was then Brent realized she hadn't removed her coat yet. It wasn't cold in the office, but he'd at first assumed she wore it to ward off the chill caused by her trip to the coffee shop. He asked her now, "Planning on going somewhere?"

Shadow gave him a puzzled look as she threw the trash in the can. "No."

"Then why don't you take your coat off?"

Heated color rushed to her cheeks, but she lifted her chin. "I don't want you to see my dress."

He sat back, prepared to be amused again. "Why not?"

"It...well..."

"Stammering, Shadow? This is different."

Her mouth tightened, then she said, "It seemed kind of cute this morning when I first dressed, but now I've decided it would be better if I kept it under wraps."

Predictably enough, Brent's gaze went to the coat concealing her dress. "Now you've intrigued me." He stood and moved closer to her. "Take it off."

It wasn't an order, more like a coaxing suggestion. Shadow shook her head. "You'll think I'm being suggestive again."

With infinite care, Brent reached out and began to undo the buttons of her soft, down-filled coat. When Shadow didn't object, holding her breath instead, he continued. She began to babble.

"It's silly, really. Just one of those joke items I'll be selling this holiday season. I wouldn't wear it anywhere but the shop, but I was in a holiday spirit this morning, and not really thinking about how it might look if someone separated me from the items I sell."

"Hush." Brent was busy giving his eyes free rein over her body. Damn, she was fine. More than fine. He had only to think of her and his muscles tensed, heated. He wanted her, and he'd have her. Soon. He parted the coat.

The dress ended well above her knees and was made of dark green knit, soft and clinging to the dips and swells of her upper body, but with a full skirt. The front, imprinted with a glitzy, decorated Christmas tree, caught and reflected the office lights off the many small sequins and buttons and beads. Brent knew it was the message printed above the fancy tree that Shadow was now feeling timid over.

Deliberately, he read it out loud. "There's Something Special under my Tree for You."

Since her body was under the tree, branches reaching across her breasts, the base ending at the notch of her thighs, Brent could understand her shyness. That she looked unbelievably enticing in the dress would only add to her dilemma. Brent skimmed the coat completely off her shoulders and down her arms, then tossed it onto the chair he'd just vacated. His hands went to her shoulders, straight and broad for a woman, emphasizing the tiny span of her waist.

"I don't ever want you to be embarrassed with me, Shadow. Promise me."

Nearly speechless, Shadow whispered, "I promise."

He caught her face in his hands. His thumbs stroked over the softness of her cheeks and chin and jaw, his fingers delving into her dark, loosely curling hair. So incredibly soft, so warm. For an endless moment he stood there like that, enjoying the differences in their sizes, the light, feminine fragrance of her, the way she watched him, her thoughts now transparent without her speaking a word. Then he released her and stepped away. "You'll have your phone number changed tomorrow?"

Shadow cleared her throat, then took several deep, openmouthed breaths. Finally she said, "Yes. I think it might be best. I've already told Kallie not to accept any more packages for me, to send them back if more should come."

"It's probably nothing to worry about, but be careful. Don't go to the parking lot alone, and keep your door locked at home."

Her slim brows lifted. "I do that anyway," she answered, obviously annoyed. "I'm not careless."

Not careless, but she was independent. "Fine." The last thing Brent had meant to do was insult her. "Let's get that damned entry form filled out then, if you really think it's necessary."

Shadow didn't give him a chance to change his mind. She hustled back behind her desk, picked up the form and smiled at him. "I've already filled in your name. Now I need your exact address."

It took only a few moments to fill out the top portion of the form. When they got to the next section, Shadow didn't bother hiding her anticipation.

"You said you're not married?"

"Am I disqualified if I say yes?"

"Availability is not a requirement for entering," Shadow said stiffly, glaring at him.

Brent chuckled. "I didn't lie. I'm not married now, nor have I ever been."

Tilting her head, Shadow asked, "Engaged? Or otherwise involved?"

"That's on the form?"

"No. It just seemed prudent to ask."

Again he laughed. "I already told you I was here alone, remember?"

"But that was when we'd just met. I thought it might be good to verify it."

His low laugh rumbled. "No. No engagement, no involvement."

Nodding, she glanced at the form, then asked, "Ever been engaged?"

"Let me guess," he said, eyeing Shadow lazily. "That's not actually on the form, either."

She shook her head, unrepentant. "Curiosity."

Brent took his time deciding whether or not he wanted to answer. Finally he figured what the hell. She may as well know how he felt about marriage. "Up until a few months ago I was engaged, but it's over now. And that was enough for me."

"Oh." The papers were laid on the desk, forgotten. "I'm sorry. I didn't mean to dredge up bad memories for you."

"You didn't. I knew I was being married for my money. I expected that. But then she informed me she didn't want children because it would ruin all her fun."

Shadow winced.

"Since having kids was the main reason *I* had wanted to marry, I ended it. And I'm not sorry that it's over. Just the opposite."

"How does she feel about it?"

Brent shrugged. "She still makes a nuisance of herself on occasion. When she found out I was moving, she took it as a sign that I was too heartbroken to stay in the same area with her."

"But you're not heartbroken?" Shadow asked.

Briefly closing his eyes, Brent said, "No. I would have made her a lousy husband, and vice versa. I'd still like to have children someday. But now I know what to look for in a wife."

"Such as?"

Apparently, as long as he was talking, Shadow was more than willing to listen. He took her by surprise when he reached across the desk to chuck her under the chin.

"For one thing, she can't be a businesswoman. Too independent. And she would have to be biddable. Someone content to be a wife and mother above all things."

Shadow smiled in understanding. "What you're looking for isn't all that unique, and one of the reasons I don't plan to marry, even though I'd love to have children, too. I even tried once—marriage, I mean. When I was only seventeen."

"Seventeen?" She'd been little more than a child. The idea was appalling.

Her eyes a little sad, she said, "I thought I wanted someone who would love me, who would put me first. Now, looking back, I think I just wanted to have sex. With my family upbringing, I couldn't do that without being married."

"What happened?" Brent was genuinely curious, which wasn't at all usual for him. A woman's personal history had never interested him before. But then, he'd never met anyone even remotely like Shadow.

"We were both young and stupid." She straightened the papers on her desk, fidgeting, then came to some hidden decision. She looked up to meet his gaze. "He also liked to smack me around. The first time it happened, I kept quiet because I hated to admit everyone was right, that I'd made a mistake. The second time, I left him, but then I let him convince me to give our marriage another try. That was a real mistake."

Brent stared at her, aware of a slow burn churning in his gut. Someone had dared to hit her? He didn't care that it was long ago, that it had less than nothing to do with him. He hadn't even known her and barely knew her now.

But none of that mattered. If she pointed the guy out today, right this second, he'd beat him into the ground. Brent drew a breath, barely getting hold of himself, and asked, "What did you do?"

"The third time he hit me I decided to get even, and when he turned his back on me that night, I surprised him with a baseball bat."

Brent sat back, amazed. "Good for you."

"I broke two of his ribs." She added with a shrug, "He never asked me to come back after that."

Through the tumultuous mix of anger and disbelief, Brent found a spot of laughter. It amazed him that she could always do that, could always amuse him, no matter what.

Her incredible eyes were still twinkling when he commented, "That was a long time ago. You haven't had the urge to give it another try?"

"Only once. When I was twenty-four, seven years after my first marriage. I almost tied that stupid knot again, but like you, I luckily found out beforehand what I was getting into. Right before, actually. Two days prior to the wedding, I discovered my fiancé going into debt on the inheritance I'd just received from my grandmother. When I walked away, he was in a killing rage, because he'd promised most of my money on investments and was seriously in debt without it. I wasn't surprised when he told me he'd only wanted me for my money, anyway. Not that I'm in your league, but Grandmother Harrison did leave me a pretty sum, enough for me to finally decide I could be independent, both personally and financially."

She tapped the pencil on the desk. "That was seven years ago. Now I'm coming to realize how much I'd like to have children of my own. Of course, in this day and age, you don't need to tie yourself into a loveless marriage to become a parent. One of my new friends, Annie, says I'm suffering my 'seven year itch' since my relationship fiascoes seem to come seven years apart." Shadow laughed. "I told her I wasn't, because I had no intention of getting married. But I am giving the parent thing some thought. As they say, my biological clock is ticking."

"You want to be a mother *now?*"

"Don't look so worried! You're not in danger of being an unwilling sperm donor. I would never get pregnant by a man without asking him first. And anyway, I'd probably do it through a clinic. You know, artificially inseminated, and all that."

Brent recovered enough to comment, "That doesn't sound like any fun."

"No, it doesn't. But then, the alternative isn't always that great, either."

Brent quirked a brow at that artless confession, then laughed when Shadow slapped her hand over her mouth. "Go on," he encouraged her, anxious to hear more.

"Forget I said that," she mumbled past her fingers. "I didn't mean to cast aspersions on the male species and their abilities."

Brent continued to smile. "I was taking it more as a challenge."

"Well, for Pete's sake, don't! I certainly didn't mean it as one."

"You make me laugh, Shadow. I like that. I like you. And as long as we're both in agreement that marriage is not a state to be devoutly sought, I think we can have some of your acclaimed *fun* together. Don't you?"

"I suppose," she agreed, but without as much enthusiasm as Brent had hoped for.

Nodding at her desk, he suggested, "Why don't we finish that contest form, then I'll help you hang the rest of your decorations."

"You don't have to do that," she assured him.

"I want to. Besides, I have nothing better to do with my time today."

"Oh. Well then, the next question is what three qualities do you look for most in a woman?"

"Attractiveness, honesty and sensuality."

Shadow stared. "That was mighty quick. You don't need time to think about it?"

Propping his elbow on the arm of his chair, he rested his chin in his palm. "Nope."

Shadow smacked her pencil down on her desk. "In that order, I suppose?"

"Certainly. If a woman isn't attractive, I wouldn't pursue her in the first place. If I got to know her, and she wasn't honest—a new criterion of mine—I wouldn't trust her, and therefore wouldn't want a relationship with her. If we started a relationship, and she was a cold fish, or a prude, there'd be no point in continuing." He shrugged.

Shadow shook her head in dismay, but then quipped, "At least you're honest about it."

"Which part are you objecting to, Shadow? It can't be the looks part, because you have to know how sexy you are."

"I'm...average. That's all."

He just smiled. "I find it hard to believe you could be a prude."

She scowled at him. "If you're trying to find out if I'm honest, the answer should be obvious. I wouldn't put out the effort necessary to lie. But what bothered me was that you didn't think a sense of humor was important. Or honor. Or generosity."

"They would have come in place after sensuality."

She rolled her eyes. "Next question—what would you consider the perfect romantic evening?"

"You mean there's only one?"

She clicked her teeth together. "You'll have to narrow it down to your favorite."

He shifted, propping his elbows on his knees, tapping his fingers together thoughtfully. When his eyes came to hold Shadow's gaze, hers darkened in reaction. He said quietly, his words deep and slow, "Being alone with a woman, the sounds of a storm outside, a warm fire. Naked, with all the time in the world ahead of us."

She looked taken aback by his deliberate and intimate use of "us." She shook her head when she realized she hadn't written his comments down, and hurried to do so, though her fingers shook slightly with the effort.

"Anything else?" Brent asked, enjoying her reaction.

"What..." Shadow cleared her throat, then tried again. "What do you like to do for fun?"

"Water ski, swim, jog." He grinned at her. "Make love."

Her pencil paused, then she quickly scribbled down his answer. "And what type of work do you do?" She was writing as she asked the final question, studiously avoiding his gaze, so she missed his expression of doubt and determination.

Beyond the bare bones, his work shouldn't interest her.

Glancing up, she said, "You gave me a business card, but it doesn't really say. Just your name and a number."

He had many businesses, and even more managers to see to those businesses. That was why he hadn't known about Shadow until boredom had forced him to come to Ohio, involving himself with his newest venture. He answered vaguely, hoping she wouldn't press. "I'm self-employed, running my own affairs. As I said earlier, I'm in real estate."

"Is it interesting?" Shadow asked as she wrote down the final information.

He looked at her bent head, the way her silky curls loosely framed her face. "More so each day."

She smiled at Brent as she folded the papers. "That's about it. All we need now is a picture. As I told you, Hot Shots here in the complex has offered to take the contestants' photos for free. We can go there now if you like, or sometime later in the week."

"If you have the time, we might as well get it over with."

THE PHOTOGRAPHER WAS very friendly—a little too friendly, Shadow thought. The woman fawned over Brent, insisting he do the shot without a shirt, and Brent, surprising Shadow, decided to oblige her. He stripped off his shirt without a hint of modesty—not that modesty was necessary. He looked incredible.

Though his hair was light brown, the hair on his chest was darker, not overly thick, but sexy. He was muscular, with broad sinewy shoulders and sculpted biceps. His abdomen was hard, lean, divided by a slender line of that dark body hair. It swirled around his navel, then disappeared into his trousers.

Shadow's heart began an erratic tattoo.

Just watching him, she flushed. Her eyes narrowed as the photographer moved Brent this way and that, taking far more shots than she had with the other contestants, her hands lingering on his bare skin. By the time they were done, Shadow wasn't feeling particularly charitable toward the woman and left without saying farewell.

Brent ignored her mood, going right to work on hanging up the remaining decorations. She insisted on helping, and took immense pleasure in each light they connected, each wreath they hung. The November weather was characteristically biting, and by the time they finished, Brent's cheekbones were red with the cold, Shadow's nose just as rosy. They went inside, laughing, and plugged in the electrical cord.

Twinkle lights wound around the outside frame of

the door and the overhang, where a huge wreath was centered. Inside, each window sported a different colored light, with a smaller wreath. The results weren't uniform or elegant, but rather festive and fun. She liked it.

Shadow was taken off guard when Brent gave her a huge hug, enfolding her in his arms and lifting her off her feet.

"Thank you. I've enjoyed myself."

Aware of Kallie watching surreptitiously, and of the few customers who gave them their attention, Shadow forced herself to pull away. She didn't want to. She wanted to pull him down to the ground and have her way with him.

She sighed. "It was fun, wasn't it? Thank you for helping."

Brent, too, noticed their audience. He caught her cold hand, led her to her office and closed the door. In the next instant, she found herself pressed up against him.

"Brent?"

"I can't wait until tonight to kiss you, Shadow." He stripped off his leather gloves and his hands came up to cup her face, his palms warm and firm. He searched her face, lingering on each small detail, and a small smile flirted with his mouth. "You're making me nuts, you know that?"

Shadow didn't have time to answer. Brent lowered his head and touched his lips to hers—not tentatively, as she would have expected a first kiss to be, but purposefully, his mouth moving over hers, his body pressing closer until she was held securely against his length.

She could hear his breathing, smell the spicy scent of

his aftershave, feel the heat and hardness of his body. Tension pulsed beneath her skin, a reaction she'd never felt before, certainly not from a simple kiss. When his tongue came out to lick over her lips, she opened, and he immediately took advantage of her quiet submission.

He tasted wonderful, she thought, curling her hands over his shoulders. Without conscious thought she closed her lips on his tongue and gently sucked.

Brent went rigid, then groaned. His body crushed closer, his breath pelting her cheek, hot and fast.

"Damn." He drew away, his eyes searching her face in near wonder. "I knew from the minute I saw you you'd be like this." He pressed his forehead to hers. "I want you, Shadow."

The words leaped from her tongue. "I want you, too. I really do."

His eyes flared, then quickly narrowed when she added with regret, "But it's too soon. I...we can't just give in to lust, Brent. I hardly know you."

He released her to shove his hands in his pockets. His sigh was long and heartfelt. "How did I know you were going to say that?"

Shadow turned her back on him. This was when he would start issuing ultimatums. She wanted to see him again, and she hadn't lied about wanting him. She did, more than she could remember wanting a man in a long, long time. But she also had deeply ingrained morals, and sleeping with a man she hardly knew went against everything she believed right and proper. Never mind that she felt she'd known him forever.

BRENT STARED AT SHADOW'S dejected stance. Withdrawn? Shadow? Not a chance. It had to be simply another part of the game she enjoyed playing. He said easily, "I better be going. I'll see you tonight at Reba's. And Shadow?"

She turned, her surprise evident.

"Don't be late."

"You still want to see me tonight?"

With a crooked grin, Brent moved toward her. Touching one finger to her soft mouth, he whispered, "Most definitely. But for my peace of mind, I think we should keep the kissing to a minimum." He laughed. "My libido just can't take all these sudden changes."

3

IT WAS TEN MINUTES after seven, and the parking lot was dark and icy cold. Shadow couldn't believe her luck, had in fact been cursing the lack of it for the past fifteen minutes.

Leaving her '66 Mustang convertible, a beauty she had always loved until now, Shadow slammed the door. It made a hollow, echoing sound across the deserted lot. The main parking area had plenty of spaces in it, but she preferred to leave her car in the back. It was less convenient to the entrance of the shops, but out of harm's way from heavy traffic and loose shopping carts.

Shadow shivered as she hurried across the pavement, holding her coat collar tight around her throat. Brent would think she'd stood him up, when that was the very last thing she'd do.

Kallie was already gone, the shop locked up. Wednesday was their only early evening, every other night of the week they were open till nine, except Sunday, when they worked only a half day. Rather than go to the bother of reopening the shop, Shadow stepped into a phone booth and closed the door so the light would come on. With numb fingers she flipped through the phone book until she found the listing for Reba's. Her teeth were chattering by the time she managed to dial the number and get an answer.

It was no surprise that she had to wait several minutes before Brent could be located. The restaurant-bar was busy in the early evening. Shadow felt such relief when Brent finally came to the phone, she actually sank back against the icy glass wall of the phone booth.

"Shadow?"

"Oh, Brent, I—I—I'm so sorry."

There was a heavy silence, then with some urgency, he demanded, "Are you all right?"

"I—I'm fine. Just f-freezing. My stupid car won't start. I d-d-didn't want you to think I'd stood you up."

Another pause, and Brent asked, "Where are you?"

"I'm outside the sh-shop. I've already locked it up for the night.... Brent?"

"I'm trying to figure out how long it'll take me to get to you. I'm still new to the area, remember."

"You don't have to—"

"Yes I do." She heard the smile in his voice. "Get in your car and lock the doors. I'll be there as quick as I can."

"I could call a cab."

"I won't argue with you, Shadow. Do as I told you and I'll be there in about five minutes."

She stared at the phone, appalled by his preemptory gall. She was more than ready to tell him what she thought, despite the bitter cold, when the phone went dead.

She returned the receiver to its cradle. Five minutes? Only if he sped. More like ten, probably. Bracing herself for the blast of bone-chilling cold, Shadow left the dubious comfort of the phone booth and hurried back to her car. She immediately locked herself inside—which she would have done with or without his instruction.

It was only about four minutes later when she saw the man approaching. But it wasn't Brent; she was certain of that. He wasn't nearly tall enough, didn't have Brent's long-legged, purposeful stride. The lighting at this section of the lot was dim, not quite reaching into the corner where she'd parked. Shadow stared, wide-eyed, as a face came into view.

The stocking cap pulled over his forehead and the scarf around his neck concealed his features until he stood directly in front of her window. He gave a broad smile and motioned for her to roll down the window.

With immense relief, Shadow recognized him.

"Hi," she called through the window.

He leaned against her door, propped his arms on the window frame and stared in at her. "You need some help?"

She shook her head. "No, everything's fine."

Again, he motioned for her to roll down the window.

The lie came easily to her lips. "I can't," she called loudly. "It's broken."

He frowned then, but said, "Open your door. I'll see if I can fix your car."

Again she lied. "There's nothing wrong with it. I'm just waiting for someone."

He seemed surprised by her answer. He straightened, stalked two steps away from the car, but quickly returned. There was a distinct scowl on his features now. "Open the door," he said again, and added, "I need to talk to you about the contest."

Shadow looked up in relief when headlights flashed across her windshield. Staring toward Brent, she said, "There's my friend now." She watched, awed by the midnight-black Jaguar XJS he drove, as he pulled up close. He parked directly in front of her, his headlights nearly blinding, and after he'd climbed from his car, she turned to open her door.

The other man was gone.

Brent looked past her. He frowned ferociously when Shadow stepped up beside him.

"A friend of yours?" he asked, his gaze still focused on the darkness beyond the lot.

"N-no." The cold immediately wrapped around her. "He was one of the contestants, actually. The pharmacist. I have no idea what he was doing here."

Brent noticed her shivers then, and quickly hustled her to his car. The motor was still running and the interior was filled with warmth. He pressed her into the passenger's seat, quickly asked her to explain what her car was doing, then gave her a firm kiss on her trembling lips. He closed the door, leaving to investigate her engine.

Shadow watched as he lifted the hood. He was very commanding, taking charge, ushering her about with a proprietary air. She couldn't decide if she should let him get away with it or not. On principle, she shouldn't. But cold as she was, she couldn't honestly say she resented his assistance.

Brent finished in only a minute. She saw him close her hood, make certain her doors were locked, then he moved his big body heavily into the seat beside her. He was silent a moment, gazing out the windshield. When he did turn to her, his expression was impassive.

"Where did the guy come from—the contestant— and what did he want?"

Something in his probing gaze drove away the last of her chills. "He just showed up," she admitted, "and asked if I needed any help. I told him I didn't, refused to open my window or my door, and told him I was waiting for someone. Why?"

"Your distributor cap is gone. Someone had to have taken it."

Incredulous, Shadow demanded, "Someone had the nerve to tamper with my car? With *my* car?"

Brent looked down at his clasped hands on the wheel. "I'd suggest we call the police, but I don't think there's anything they could do about it." Then he looked up again. "I just hate leaving your car here overnight. A classic like that, someone might feel tempted to make off with it."

Shadow considered that, then suggested, "I could have the security guys keep an eye on it for me. They're really nice, so I don't think they'll mind."

Brent slanted her a look. "Do you know everyone around here?"

"I'm friendly," she said with a shrug. "And when I first leased the shop, it needed a lot of decorating done to it. I spent some pretty late hours here. The security guys made a habit of checking up on me. Still do sometimes. I only recently put the finishing touches on everything, like the window blinds the day I, ah, met you." She flushed, remembering that day. She rushed on, saying, "They're nice men, but they flatly refused to enter the contest."

He made a sound somewhere between laughter and irritation. "Have you solicited every guy in the area?"

"Yeah, pretty much." She grinned at him. "I was about out of hope when I found you. Now I only need two more." He touched her cheek, the corner of her mouth. "Do you have a number for the security people?"

"Yes."

"Are you hungry, or would you rather I just take you home?"

"Well," she said, feeling suddenly shy, "I was thinking, if you hadn't already eaten, we could pick up a pizza and take it to my place. I could call security from there."

Brent went very still beside her. "Your place?"

"It isn't an invitation for anything more than pizza. I...I'm trusting you."

Slowly nodding, Brent answered just as quietly. "I can handle that. Pizza sounds great." Then he reached across the seat to take her hand, and to Shadow's immense pleasure, he didn't release it until they had reached the pizza parlor and had to get out to order.

She wanted to be with Brent, but she didn't want to sit in a crowded restaurant and look at him across a table. She was willing to trust her instincts, and that meant trusting Brent, because she felt safe with him. Even stranger than that, she was relaxed in his company, comfortable with him as a man. There was no way she was going to let such an appealing aberration pass her by.

OPENING THE WINE was a mistake. Brent had purchased it, along with the large, loaded pizza, while she'd gone to the ladies' room to refresh herself. She'd been nervous over her decision to take him to her home, and had needed a few private moments to collect herself. When she'd returned, Brent had already paid and was waiting for her by the door.

He pointed out his house on the way and Shadow noted she would pass it each time she traveled to or from work. It was every bit as massive and impressive as she'd imagined it to be. Brent had, predictably, shrugged off her awe. What had surprised Shadow, though, was that he was just as impressed with her much smaller home. It, too, was very old, but not nearly as large or in as excellent shape. But she was working on that.

"Did you do all these renovations by yourself?"

She puffed up with pride. "For the most part. My father was a handyman. He taught me quite a bit about repairs and upkeep. But you can see I have a long way to go yet."

Sitting in the kitchen, a large airy room with solid oak cabinets and an ancient, rustic stove, Shadow pointed out the need for new wainscoting and chair rails. Wallpaper would be the last thing she purchased.

A fat, bright red candle burned on the round, pedestal-base oak table between them. Shadow watched, slightly light-headed, as Brent refilled her wineglass. The pale, golden shimmer of the candle shone through the crimson wine, illuminating it, fascinating her. She hadn't particularly liked the taste of it at first, but had been hesitant to admit that to Brent. He was more sophisticated than her and plainly assumed wine was necessary with pizza.

Now, however, after three full glasses, and the resulting lethargic unconcern, Shadow was beginning to wonder if she should tell him the sorry truth. She was, plainly put, a down-home girl and painfully unsophisticated.

Shoving the empty pizza box aside, Brent caught her limp hand and tugged her from her seat. "Show me the rest of your house."

Blinking at his handsome face, Shadow noticed things she hadn't noticed before: the way his light brown hair curled slightly over his forehead, despite the perfection of the cut, and his rugged beard shadow, now apparent at this hour of the evening. And the way his green eyes seemed so warm and mellow, so...caressing. Swaying toward him, Shadow whispered, "Kiss me again first."

Brent drew up short at her request, but only for a moment. He lowered his head and touched his mouth discreetly to the corner of her parted lips.

Shadow sighed in disappointment. Her heart shuddered, her breathing quickened, but mostly in anticipation. His kiss was over with before she even finished reacting to it.

His smile was gentle now, the grip on her arm firm.

Turning her away with a small chuckle, Brent reminded her, "Your house? I would like to see the rest of it. You'd made me think it was small, but it's not. Not at all. How many rooms do you have?"

It was impossible to hide her disgruntled irritation with him and his avuncular kiss, but she tried. "There are five bedrooms, four upstairs. But I haven't done a thing up there yet. It's all locked up, and it'll probably stay that way until summer."

"I love your dining room and living room."

"Thank you." She sent him a sappy smile. "I refinished the floors myself. There was this musty old carpet hiding the hardwood floors. Some of the flooring had to be replaced along the outside wall, but other than that, it was in good shape, just needing a thorough polishing."

As SHADOW EXTOLLED the magnificence of her house, Brent made appropriate sounds of appreciation, but his attention was on her. She wasn't walking quite steadily, and she couldn't seem to take her eyes off him for more than a few moments.

Shadow grinned at him suddenly. "My room is the only one I have completely finished. Would you like to see it?"

He hesitated in answering, but only for a second. "Lead the way."

The living room and dining room were on the left side of the house, a curved, polished wood stairway gracing the middle. The kitchen and a small guest bathroom were situated at the back, and to the right was a family room with a huge, full wall stone fireplace. Behind that, adjacent to the kitchen, was the room Shadow had claimed as her own.

Double doors opened into a spacious, high-ceilinged room, with an ornately etched cornice framing the walls. Patterned rugs in pastel shades of yellow, green and blue covered the floor. The down-filled comforter on her bed was plush and colored the palest yellow, with deep green floral throw pillows tossed near the high headboard.

The room abounded in plants, hanging from the corners, set on the sills of the three high, narrow windows and placed on every available surface. Vine printed wallpaper covered three of the walls, but behind her bed there was a thin, gauzy, pale yellow material, parted to hang on either side, framing her bed and giving it prominence in the room. All the furniture was antique, heavy and dark. It was a mix of feminine and masculine, beautifully done.

Brent wandered about the room, idly touching various picture frames, small jewelry cases and the abundance of womanly items: hair bows, earrings, perfume bottles. He came to a closed door, not the type to open to a closet, and turned to Shadow.

"You can go in. It's my bathroom, another room I'm real proud of. Maybe my favorite room in the house."

Shadow remained by the door where they'd first entered. To Brent's discerning eye, she appeared to be propping herself up against the wall.

She waited for his reaction to the bathroom, watching him closely. What wasn't to like? The antiquated tub sat on clawed feet, two narrow wooden Shaker tables beside it holding an array of bath oils, thick towels and a few lush plants. Directly over the tub she'd built a ledge, trimmed in brass and nearly covered with different sized colored candles that gave off a blend of subtle fragrances. He thought the room downright decadent, but it also showed what a traditionalist she was.

Everything—sink, tub and ceramic tiles—was white. The wide window on the back wall, glazed and opaque, was covered with only a thin, pale sheer to allow sunlight, or moonlight, to shine into the room. Brent stared at the tub for a long time, imagining her in it, naked, with each and every candle glowing around her.

He turned just in time to see her tip up her glass, gulping the remainder of her wine, which she had carried with her. He watched her with a slight smile as he approached.

"These rooms are very much like you, Shadow. Bright and open. A little different, but pleasantly so. And very inviting." He took the wineglass from her hand and set it on her nightstand. "You've turned bathing into a hedonistic experience, sweetheart."

Her eyes widened at the endearment. She gave a

slight groan and swayed toward him, her gaze on his mouth, which Brent couldn't keep from tilting up in an amused grin.

He caught her shoulders and held her away, his sigh long, but indulgent. "You don't drink very often, do you, Shadow?"

"Never." She nestled close to his chest and he allowed it, even stroked her soft hair. "You smell delicious," she said, rubbing her nose against the front of his shirt, then upward, against his throat.

Brent went rigid as his body reacted predictably to her innocent—intoxicated—seduction. It wasn't easy, and his hands even shook, but he caught her shoulders again and moved her back so her body could no longer lean into his.

"You're going to force me," he said with a growl, "to prove how noble I can be."

Ignoring his proffered nobility, Shadow ran her small, warm hands over his chest, down his ribs. His breath caught as she skimmed her fingers over his abdomen, but she stopped there. He was equally disappointed and relieved.

"Brent," she implored in a whisper, "kiss me."

She didn't wait for him to comply, but grasped the hair at the back of his neck and pulled his face down so she could reach his mouth. Brent was half laughing, half groaning at his predicament, until her soft breasts came up against his chest and her belly pressed into his erection.

He wasn't a damn saint, Brent told himself, giving up all at once and kissing her as he'd wanted to since he'd first spotted her in the window. He forced her mouth open, sank his tongue deep, tasting her, devouring her. She was an irresistible temptation and he was tired of resisting.

She groaned with appreciation. "You make me crazy, Brent," she said between kissing his throat, his ear, his mouth again. "I've never felt like this before."

"It's the wine," he rasped harshly, struggling between guilt and lust. But Shadow only shook her head.

Taking his words as an excuse, not the complaint they had actually been, she whispered, "It's not just a physical thing, you know? I mean, all those books that proclaim fireworks and explosions and..." Her hands curled into the front of his sweater, fisting in the material. She shook him slightly, or at least tried to, and said, "I'm feeling them, Brent!"

He almost laughed at her turbulent expression. He did untangle her fingers from his clothes and carefully pinned her arms to her sides. If he wasn't so damned aroused, the situation might actually have been funny. "Shadow, we have to stop now. I'm only here for the pizza, remember?" He smoothed her dark hair, continually drawn by the silkiness of it. "If you keep kissing me like that, I'm going to lose my head. And unfortunately, I have the feeling you'll never forgive me if I take advantage of you tonight."

"Oh, Brent, please," she said, "take advantage of me." Her look was earnest and filled with worry. "It might not ever be like this again."

Damn, how could one eccentric little woman twist him inside out? "Sweetheart, the feelings aren't going anywhere. When you're ready, you'll feel them again, I promise."

Abruptly moving away from him, she asked, horrified, "You don't want me?"

Brent ran a hand over his face. He should give her

what she wanted, nobility be damned. But the truth was he didn't want to alienate her and possibly lose her so soon simply because he couldn't control himself. Even now she was swaying where she stood, the wine affecting her more than he would have thought possible. She trembled, her cheeks flushed, her eyes heavy. All in all, she made a very enticing picture standing there before him in the Christmas tree dress and red tights.

And she looked so damned forlorn, as if she really believed he didn't want her. If she took a closer look at his lap, she'd find the evidence she wanted. But he was a man, not a boy, and he had himself firmly in control. Always.

It was that thought that made up his mind. He could use this situation, as absurd as it seemed, to show Shadow a thing or two about his character. Come the morning, she would no longer doubt who was in control.

She whispered suddenly, "I'm in an agony of suspense, Brent. What are you thinking?"

"I'm thinking," he said gently, "that you're drunk."

She licked her lips. "It's true, I don't drink much. But it wouldn't have happened this way with any other man, I'm sure of that." She stared up him, her big brown eyes slumberous, heated. "There's just...something about you."

Feeling very pleased with her statement, Brent said, "I'm glad," and he hugged her close. She misunderstood his intent and cried out in relief, squeezing her arms around his neck in a near choke hold.

Carefully, Brent gauged his actions and her responses as he took her mouth again. She tasted sweet, and he wanted to kiss her all over. He'd prove himself trustworthy, a man in control, if it killed him.

She accepted the thrust of his tongue and gave him her own. He held her steady for his well-planned onslaught. When her body moved against his, he countered her movements, making her heartbeat race and her breathing hitch. His erection throbbed against her soft belly. He stroked her slender back, down her spine, until he could fill his hands with her firm backside. He lifted her a bit, caressing her, holding her against him.

Their mingled groans echoed loudly in the silent room. Slowly, Brent began backing her toward her bed. He wanted her—as much or more than she wanted him.

The bed was large and raised high off the floor so that the backs of her thighs bumped into the firm mattress. Brent didn't lower her right away, as she seemed anxious for him to do. Instead, he went to work on the zipper at the back of her dress, teasing her by lowering it slowly, letting the tips of his fingers graze her spine as he did so.

His mouth never left hers for long; he couldn't seem to stop kissing her, touching her. He knew his touted discipline was precarious at best.

He pushed her dress over her shoulders and down her arms, bunching it around her wrists. When Shadow went to pull it free, Brent stopped her, holding her hands and watching the small thrill in her eyes as she realized she was caught, her arms pinned to her sides. He had a feeling she'd never have allowed such a thing if she hadn't been tipsy. But the fact was she had drunk too much, and now she was at his mercy.

He had plenty to spare, but he also intended to show her a thing or two.

Brent stared down at her, then carefully guided her to lie flat on the bed. His chest rose and fell with his deep breathing and his hands trembled with need. He visually explored her exposed skin, her throat, the soft swells of her full breasts above the red demi-bra she wore. Lowering himself, he half reclined on her, his hips between her legs, which still dangled over the side of the bed, his upper body supported by his bent arms. He dipped his head, letting her feel first the heat of his breath, then the moist touch of his tongue on her skin.

"You're a tease, Brent Bramwell," she whispered breathlessly.

Using his teeth, he lightly nibbled where her pulse fluttered at the base of her throat. "I fully intend," he whispered, "to get as much enjoyment out of this as I can under the circumstances. So don't think to rush me."

"What circumstances?" she asked him, but he easily distracted her. Her eyes closed languorously when he moved his attention to her ear. She squirmed a little as he licked, teased, and her breath sighed out brokenly.

He cupped her breast and her small nipple grew taut beneath the layer of silky material. Using his thumb, Brent flicked and rubbed, and she arched, trying to align their bodies, but he wouldn't allow it.

Slowly, he dragged the narrow straps of her bra down her upper arms. Damn, he wanted to see her, all of her. He tugged the bra down the rest of the way until it caught beneath her breasts. Her nipples were dark pink, puckered tight. He took only a moment to nuzzle his face into her softness before he closed his mouth over one sensitive peak.

Shadow jerked sharply. "Brent!"

"What?" He licked, tugged carefully with his teeth. "Tell me, sweetheart."

"It's...almost too much," she gasped.

"It's not enough." He switched to her other breast, drawing her deep. He used one hand to soothe the nipple he'd just abandoned, while the other grasped her leg high on her thigh, urging it up and over his hip.

The heat was nearly unbearable, pulsing beneath his skin, gathering between his legs. More than anything, he wanted to be inside her.

Shadow redoubled her efforts to get her arms free, but now her bra added to her restraints.

"Shh," he said, leaning back to look at her breasts.

"Brent, don't leave me."

"How are you feeling, sweetheart?"

She struggled for breath. "My head is whirling, but it's not the wine."

He felt grim, and determined. "Of course not."

"It's not! It's you and what you're doing to me, how you're kissing me."

"This?" he asked, and gave another sweet sucking kiss to her nipple, while flattening his palm on her small belly.

"*Yes.*" Her legs moved restlessly beneath him.

He'd never known a woman to be so wild, so urgent and demanding. He didn't dare undress her; he knew he didn't have that much restraint.

Breathing hard, he shoved down her tights until he had free access to her body. It was nearly his undoing.

Hot. And wet and so damned soft he knew he had to hurry or he'd never make it. Her curls were dark here, too, glossy, and she gasped at his first touch, then went perfectly still.

He tested her with gentle touches that only caused her to demand more. She gave a hoarse groan, lifting her hips when he slid his middle finger deep inside her. She was so tight, so silky wet and ready for him. He could just imagine...

No, he'd better not. He could already feel the clench of her muscles, the tiny spasms. Damn, he'd barely touched her and she was as far gone as he. Her response was surprising, and arousing.

Concentrating on her every reaction, Brent began to caress her, carefully, calculating each move and her reaction to it, discovering what pleased her most. It wasn't long before he had what he wanted.

"Ahh, Brent." Her words were strangled, rasped out through parted lips.

"That's it, honey." He felt on the verge of his own climax, every muscle in his body taut and straining. "Open your eyes, Shadow, and look at me."

She did and he felt seared to his bones by the heat in her gaze. Keeping his eyes locked with hers, he squeezed another finger inside her, then used his thumb to stroke her where she needed his touch most. It was incredible, watching her as she climaxed. Her body tensed, trembled; her eyes were wild on his face, her hips straining against his fingers. It took all his control to keep from coming himself. He kissed her deeply, taking her cries into his own mouth, holding her close until the very last shudder had ended, until she went limp and drowsy.

His heart still galloped, but hers had settled into a slow, deep rhythm. Brent levered himself upward, taking in her sprawled form with triumph and possession. Shadow didn't move, not even when he sat up fully at her side.

She was sound asleep, partly from the wine, most likely, but he was taking a great deal of the credit after the screaming climax he'd just given her. Brent couldn't ever remember feeling quite so satisfied, especially given the fact that his erection still throbbed and his muscles were bunched and rigid.

He was a little chagrined when Shadow didn't stir even as he pulled her arms free from the confines of her clothing. She looked sexy, but also adorable, her soft, slightly swollen lips still parted, her thick lashes lying heavily against her flushed cheeks.

Both her legs hung limply over the side of the bed, one shoe still dangling from her toes. Brent smiled, a strange tenderness invading his chest, making him shake his head at the irony of the situation. It was the first time he'd ever undressed a woman who was dead to the world and unable to appreciate his efforts.

But seeing her, all of her—that was something. She had pale skin, so smooth, her belly soft, her thighs sleek. For a long time he merely looked at her, and did his best to ignore those emotions he couldn't put a name to.

No doubt about it, he had a long night ahead of him. But he fully intended to be on hand when Shadow awoke in the morning. In fact, he wouldn't miss it for the world.

SHADOW HAD ALWAYS BEEN a sound sleeper. When she was a little girl, her father had teased her, saying he could drop her down the steps once she was asleep, and she wouldn't even flicker an eyelid. But she also woke with no remnants of lethargy to cloud her brain. She simply opened her eyes and was completely alert. She did that now, but once awake, she didn't move.

Something wasn't right, and it wasn't just that she was naked, an unusual sleeping state for her. She always bundled up in warm thermal pajamas to stay warm. She was warm now. Toasty even.

But she wasn't alone, a fact verified by the hairy leg thrown so casually over her own and the heavy, muscled arm possessively circling her chest, just beneath her breasts. Even in the very dim morning light, she recognized Brent.

Her stomach flip-flopped and she froze.

In a rush, she remembered quite a bit of last night: the wine, the kissing. The significant other things that had happened. But she didn't remember undressing and going to bed. It wasn't possible that she'd fallen asleep before Brent could satisfy himself, was it? Yet, that must be what had happened, since she had absolutely no recollection of making love.

Shadow was so deep into her thoughts it was a miracle that the tiny motion by the window caught her attention at all. But it did, and when she turned her head, she could have sworn she saw the murky outline of a face. She quite naturally screamed before she could stop herself.

Like an alley cat, Brent leaped from the bed, his hair on end, his eyes wild, his body in a defensive stance.

Forgetting the possibility of a Peeping Tom for one single moment, Shadow stared at Brent's naked body. Good grief, she'd gone to sleep and missed out on *that?*

"What?" Brent demanded, his eyes still wide, his head turning this way and that in his effort to locate the cause of her scream. "What the hell's the matter?"

"I'm sorry," Shadow replied, chagrined for a number of reasons while her gaze remained on his hard belly—and below. "I've never actually screamed before." She managed to drag her attention to his face, but it wasn't easy. "I think there was someone peeking in the window."

Brent's brows lowered in a furious frown. He stalked to the window, giving Shadow a back view that made her flush, and peered out. "All I see is an empty side yard and the brick wall of your neighbor's house."

She cleared her throat. He was gloriously naked, so speech wasn't exactly easy. "I'm pretty sure I saw—"

Without letting her finish, he went around the bed in a determined stomp and growled, "Stay here."

Shadow watched, incredulous, as Brent left the room. "Ohmigod." She grabbed the comforter around herself and stared after him. "Brent, you're naked!"

He never slowed, just waved her back, and she sank into the bed in disbelief. He was gone only a minute, but it was long enough. The second he strode back into the bedroom, she threw a pillow at him...and missed.

"Are you nuts?" she yelled, swinging another pillow at his head. "You don't try to confront an intruder buck naked! What would you have done if he'd jumped on you?"

Brent dodged the second pillow, then caught it in midair and tossed it back at Shadow before coming onto the bed with her. "There wasn't anyone out there," he informed her, and wrestled her down, ignoring her fit of anger. She fought him only halfheartedly. After all, they were both nude and there was a lot of skin touching. When he finally had her pinned to the mattress, he kissed her.

He smelled wonderful, she thought, musky and male. Early morning beard stubble abraded her skin, but she didn't mind. She was too busy feeling him, all of him. His skin was hot, even after his brief glimpse out the back door, and his arms felt like steel. He was so hard all over.

Brent ended the kiss, but came back for several more, pressing tiny, biting nibbles on her lips, her chin, her jaw. His voice was very deep and rough when he asked, "Are you completely sober this morning?"

Shadow frowned, not understanding, but Brent kept running his palms up and down her body and she couldn't really think straight. "I'm sober."

He kissed her again, his tongue invading leisurely to stroke over her own, then soothe gently over her bottom lip. "And do you still want me?"

"Oh, Brent. I'm so sorry." This, she thought, was the epitome of the awkward "morning after." "I can't imagine how I fell asleep last night. You must think I'm awful."

"Actually," he said, licking her throat and driving her crazy, "you were spectacular."

Shadow frowned again, and this time she didn't let Brent distract her. "What do you mean?"

"I mean you're beautiful when you come. Wild and natural. That was all I wanted last night, sweetheart." He smiled at her, his expression...smug. "I could have awakened you if I'd really wanted to. But I was content to wait until this morning."

"You mean to tell me," Shadow inquired with false calm, "that you had no intention of making love to me last night, despite what you did...what I let you do...what happened?"

Grinning at the way she stammered, wrongly assuming she suffered belated shyness from having been so abandoned, Brent felt safe in teasing her. "I'm not a teenager, Shadow. I can control myself, and you, when necessary. But I have to admit, it wasn't easy getting to sleep last night with your warm, sweet body next to me."

He started to lean down to kiss her again, but Shadow stiffened her arms to hold him off. "You undressed me? After I was asleep?"

"All I did was pull off your tights and shove your dress the rest of the way down. You were already nearly there, if you remember."

Her shove sent him sprawling on the bed beside her. In a heartbeat she gained her feet, the comforter wrapped around her. "You big jerk! You...you *toyed* with me!"

Throwing one arm over his eyes in exasperation, Brent said, "I don't believe this."

"I don't either!" Shadow couldn't remember ever being so embarrassed in her life. "How could you?"

He dropped his arm to glare at her. Lifting himself up on one elbow, he said, "You were drunk, damn it! Should I have taken advantage of you?"

"That's like saying you haven't stolen the apple if you only take one bite of it! Since you did me, you should have done you, too."

"Did you? *Did you?* What the hell does that mean?"

Through clenched teeth, Shadow said, "You know what it means."

"You were half-drunk and crawling all over me. You'd said earlier that it was too damn soon to make love, so rather than take advantage of your condition, and not being a bastard who'd leave you unsatisfied, I took care of it."

Shadow stared at him. She'd been crawling all over him? It was even worse than she'd thought.

Brent shrugged. "I *assumed* you'd be grateful."

"Grateful," she all but sputtered.

"I sure as hell didn't think you'd get mad."

She tipped her chin stubbornly. "Why would you start something you had no intention of finishing? That's just not...male." Never in her life had she known a man to give without taking, not where sex was concerned.

Brent lost his temper. Rising from the bed in a quiet rage, he stalked toward her. His words were low and mean, his brows drawn into a fierce scowl. "I did finish it, or are you going to tell me you faked it?"

His insulting suggestion nearly made her hair stand on end. "As if I would."

Her quick agreement earned her a dubious double take. His mouth opened, closed. Finally, he said, "Exactly. So tell me, lady. What the hell are you complaining about?"

Men could be so dense. "You got nothing out of it."

Eyes blazing, he tweaked her chin and said, "I watched you come. I heard you yell and felt you tighten on my fingers. That's a lot. A hell of a lot, actually. I'd do it again in a heartbeat if you weren't being so damn unreasonable. So don't tell me what I did or didn't get out of our little interlude, because I have a feeling you don't know jack about men, and worse, you're judging me by some jerks from long ago. I don't like it."

Shadow watched him, openmouthed and for once speechless, as he turned and stalked away. Well, hell.

4

HAVING HELPED HIMSELF to coffee, Brent was at the kitchen table when Shadow entered. Sunlight now poured through the windows, making the kitchen appear warm and cozy. She was fresh from her shower, properly dressed and still chagrined.

Brent glanced up. "Feeling better?"

Knowing there was no hope for it, she blurted, "I'm sorry."

One tawny brow arched up a good inch. "Oh? What for, exactly?" Brent waved her into a chair and stood to pour her a cup of coffee. His cordial good spirits put her further on edge. She had a very hard time figuring him out.

Swallowing a good dose of caffeine before answering, she admitted, "You were right. I really had no reason to complain. I'm just not used to waking up with naked men in my bed."

He grinned at that.

"And," she added, liking his grin even less than his good humor, "it's especially strange for a naked man to be in my bed and not want to...well, have sex."

Brent studied her over the rim of his coffee mug as he took his own cautious sip. "I already accepted that last night wasn't something you do on a regular basis. But let's get clear on this. I did want you very much. I still do, for that matter."

He sat at the table, at his leisure, a man without a care. Her disgruntlement amplified. "You show remarkable restraint."

"Should I throw you over my shoulder, Shadow? Drag you off to bed and do the caveman routine?"

Shadow stared into her coffee cup. He'd actually hurt her feelings, she admitted to herself. They'd slept together in celibate bliss and it made her feel less than appealing. "Of course not. But don't you think I'd know the difference between real desire and wine-induced lust?"

He didn't answer. *In for a penny*, she thought. She curled her fingers around the warm coffee mug and forged onward. "Had I been with anyone other than you, Brent, it wouldn't have happened. But I was with you, and I wanted you. You're...special. What you make me feel is special." She let out her breath and added, "That's why I'm upset."

Her admission both pleased and perplexed Brent. He'd had time to think while she dressed in fresh jeans and a pastel pink sweatshirt. It said H.S.A. State. Brent had no idea what that meant, and at the moment, he didn't care.

Waking to a scream had thrown him all off balance. He'd assumed Shadow had a bit of a hangover, which had caused her to mistake a shadow for a man, but he didn't say as much. He wasn't a complete idiot. And besides, she didn't act hungover. Other than that startling scream and her grumbling because they hadn't made love, she was the same as ever. Which meant she was as difficult as ever to understand.

He, however, felt forever changed. He wasn't used to such an amalgam of feelings where women were concerned, but Shadow affected him, no way around it. He had only to look at her with her fresh scrubbed face, her hair damp from her shower, and he wanted her, fiercely. Control? Ha. His control was so thin it was laughable. His body had been semihard all morning and he didn't think the condition would go away anytime soon.

But it was, strangely enough, more than just lust, though the lust was strong enough to bring him low. He also wanted to talk to her, to hold her. Feeling her next to him throughout the night had been torturous, and oddly satisfying.

"The problem," Shadow said, interrupting his thoughts, "is that for the first time, despite the wine, I lost my senses. I've never done that. It's a bit disappointing that you...didn't, too. I'll admit I don't like it." She made a face. "It sort of leaves things unbalanced."

"You're mad because I didn't lose control?" He felt disbelief and a touch of annoyance. Every woman he'd ever known had valued his control, relied on it, counted on it. He also felt a surge of hunger so strong it shook him. She was so open about wanting him, how could he not return the favor?

"There it is." She looked as confused as he felt. "You leave me at a disadvantage, which is a place I've been too many times with men. I swore I wouldn't ever let that happen again."

Running his hand roughly through his already rumpled hair, Brent fell back in his chair, resigned. "So you don't want to see me again?" Not that it mattered. He had no intention of walking away just yet, and since he held her lease, he'd have plenty of reasons to see her if she did try to end things.

"I'm not sure." She took a deep breath, warning him

that he wouldn't like what he was about to hear. And he was right.

"But I'm not going to sleep with you until I've had time to think about this, to figure it out."

Talk about a plan backfiring... With a humorless laugh, Brent stood. "First you raise hell because I didn't take you, and now you're saying you may not even want me to. You're fickle, Shadow."

"I'm just trying to—"

"I know what you're trying to do, honey. You want to run the show, to call all the shots. Fine. But don't expect me to sit around waiting for you to make up your mind how to do it."

Her big brown eyes were direct, but also solemn. She wasn't going to give an inch. "If that's how you want it."

She had the upper hand and he hated it. In fact, he wouldn't tolerate it. He gulped down the last of his coffee and said matter-of-factly, "Go get your coat. We'll see what we can do about your car."

Uncertainty, and if he wasn't mistaken, hopefulness, settled over her. "My coat?"

"Yes. It's cold outside, and it snowed again last night." When a slow, impish smile lit her face, Brent felt his chest constrict. Unfulfilled lust, he decided, nothing more. "I'll take you by the auto parts store and we can pick up a distributor cap."

She scampered out of her chair. "I'll just be a minute."

When she turned to leave, Brent finally read the words on the back of her sweatshirt. His laugh took her by surprise.

"I think I'm the one who should be wearing that," he said.

"What?"

"Your shirt. H.S.A. State? I didn't understand what the initials stood for until now." He read aloud, still chuckling, "'The State of Heightened Sexual Arousal.' Very catchy."

Shadow's smile went crooked. "It's a very big seller."

"I can imagine." With Shadow in the vicinity, every male for miles probably knew that state.

All humor vanished when they stepped outside. Brent was the first to notice the footprints in the snow. They led around the house, leaving the walkway occasionally, where it was obvious someone had approached the house to peer inside the windows. When he'd looked out the door earlier, it had been too dark to notice them. But now he saw there was even one window where the ice had been scratched off, to give a clearer view.

"I told you I saw someone," Shadow reminded him, trudging behind him as he retraced each print. They made a marked path at the side of the house, then headed toward the street. Brent broke into a trot when he realized they led to his car, which he'd left parked on the curb in front.

His curses should have melted the snow. A single, long, deeply etched scratch ran from the front fender to the back. Shadow looked nearly sick, and Brent went rigid with rage.

"Oh, Brent. I'm so sorry."

"I'll get the bastard," he said through his teeth, "don't worry about that." His anger shifted to near fear when he realized the ramifications of the damage. "This is too much of a coincidence to ignore. Your secret admirer, probably the guy from last night, has crossed the line from annoying to dangerous. Phone calls are one thing, breaching someone's privacy and damaging their property is too damn much."

She caught her hands together. "You really think it's him? But that doesn't make any sense. It's just been a few calls, a few small gifts."

"And a missing distributor cap."

Her brown eyes were grim, a little scared. "You don't think those are unrelated incidents?"

Brent would have liked to reassure her, but he couldn't. "You have the address and phone number of the guy who was in the parking lot last night?" he asked.

"Yes. When he entered the contest, he filled out all the papers you did."

"I think he's the one."

She looked around her quiet street, her cheeks pale, her mouth tight. "We should call the police."

"Damn right." He took her arm, his mind made up. "And from now on, until this is resolved, I'm keeping a very close eye on you—whether you want to see me or not.

SHADOW COULDN'T DECIDE which was worse, having someone harass her or having Brent constantly glaring over her shoulder. She wouldn't have minded the latter so much, except that was all he did.

He hadn't kissed her again, made no reference to their one night together and acted more like an over-anxious parent than an interested male. Shadow was fed up with it.

Her secret admirer was still a secret. Despite Brent's assumption that Chad Moreland, the pharmacist who'd entered her contest, was the guilty man, it hadn't worked out that way.

Brent had ranted and raved at the police station when he was told Chad had a solid alibi for his whereabouts the day Brent's car had been vandalized. And sending flowers and cards wasn't a crime, even if they could prove he'd done so, which they couldn't. Chad denied any association with Shadow, other than participation in her contest. She was embarrassed to have accused him, and Brent was furious that he didn't have answers. He wasn't convinced Chad was innocent, but there was nothing the police could do.

What had further enraged Brent was the warning the officer felt compelled to give him. Brent couldn't touch Chad and shouldn't threaten him. A restraining order was out of the question, unless they could provide proof of identification that Chad was the man who'd been at her house. They couldn't. The only thing Chad had done was offer Shadow assistance the night her car wouldn't start. He'd been on his way to a party, he'd said, and it had turned into an all-nighter. He even seemed hurt by Shadow's accusations. She didn't know what to think.

"Are you ready to go yet?" Brent asked from the office doorway.

Shadow looked up from her inventory check. Brent stood there, dressed in black jeans, a charcoal-gray pullover and a black leather jacket. It was an effort to draw her eyes away from him. Although it had been little more than a week since the fateful night that had sent everything awry, it felt like months to Shadow. She couldn't sleep for wanting to touch him again, to kiss him and have him kiss her back, to...

But she'd ended all that herself. If Brent was still interested, he was evidently waiting for her to start things back up. Damn, but she hated getting herself into these impossible situations.

"I'll be ready in just a moment," she answered with a sigh.

"Any calls today? Any gifts?"

Same old song, same old dance, she thought. "Not a thing." She closed her books and went to get her coat from the rack. "We probably overreacted."

"Don't sound so hopeful. I think it's more likely my presence has scared him off, but I'm not taking any chances."

She already knew that. Brent proved to be a most ardent protector. So far, he hadn't once behaved as she'd expected.

He took her arm as they started out the door and even that innocent touch had Shadow's pulse leaping. His hands were so large, so strong and always so warm. Turning her face up to his, she suggested, "Why don't we celebrate his disappearance? We could stop and eat somewhere. Or maybe—"

Brent interrupted her, his jaw tensing in a noticeable way. "I already have plans."

"Oh." Her heart sank. Their relationship, started with such intimacy, had dwindled to a friendship; Brent wanted her safe, but that's all he wanted. She should have been pleased with his concern, but instead dejection weighed her down.

Brent slanted her a look as he opened her car door and helped her inside. Leaning one arm against the roof, oblivious to the snow that had gathered there, he explained gently, "I usually go home to see my parents on Thanksgiving. But I canceled this year, so they're coming here for a short visit. They're arriving tonight."

Her heart sputtered back to life. *His parents.* That was definitely preferable to another woman!

"They won't stay long," he explained, "because they need to be back in Chicago before Thanksgiving. My grandparents and other relatives usually show up there for the holidays."

Shadow knew immediately why Brent had changed his plans. Guilt swamped her. "This is ridiculous, Brent. You shouldn't miss a family gathering just for me."

It was the first tender look he'd given her since the night he'd stayed at her house. He said gently, "I didn't feel up to going all the way to Chicago, anyway. And my parents were curious to see where I'm living, so they're actually looking forward to coming here."

He tried to make light of it, to make her feel better, but it only made her feel worse. "Does that mean you'll be all alone on Thanksgiving?"

"Shadow..."

She didn't let him finish. "You could come home with me. My parents would love to meet you."

Brent stepped away from the car. "I don't think that'd be a good idea."

His immediate rejection felt like a slap, but she hid her hurt. The last thing she wanted was his pity. "If you change your mind, just let me know."

"I'll do that." Brent closed her door, then waited until she'd started her car before going to his own. As usual, he followed her to her house. There was no sign of Chad or anyone else hanging around.

Shadow unlocked the front door, reached inside to turn on the wall switches, then turned back to the street, waving to Brent. He returned her wave, but didn't pull away. He waited in his car, watching, until she finally closed and locked the door.

As she shrugged out of her coat, she pressed the button on her answering machine to receive her messages. Listening to her friend Annie extend an invitation for holiday shopping, Shadow almost missed the note on the floor.

She picked it up, and one quick look made her knees weak. Written in a childish scrawl, it said, "No other man can replace me. I'm patient, so I'll wait. For now. Yours, always."

He'd been in her house, was Shadow's first horrified thought. She ran from door to door, checking the locks and thankfully finding each secure. Her heart was still hammering when she realized the note could have easily been slipped through the mail slot, which was right over the telephone table. She took several deep breaths to calm herself and then a new thought came to mind.

If Brent found out, he'd never stop hovering. She was already disrupting his Thanksgiving holiday; how could she impose further? Why he felt it his duty to protect her in the first place, Shadow couldn't fathom. It was apparent he no longer wanted her sexually— even his superhuman control wasn't that strong. And they'd only known each other a little over a week, so he couldn't feel obligated out of long association.

He owed her nothing. But she knew instinctively that he'd become even more diligent if he found out about the note.

It was ironic, since she was the one who'd put him off, but with each new day, Shadow wanted him more. Brent was strong and stubborn and proud. And protective.

She admired him too much to keep him at her side

when he didn't really want her, simply because he suffered some outdated notions of male obligation. The police weren't overly concerned, so she wouldn't be, either. She wasn't a helpless female. She'd been taking care of herself for a long time and she liked it that way. Any relationship she had would have to be reciprocal. Her sense of independence demanded that much.

Giving the note a scathing glare, she picked up the phone and called the police. The same officer who'd taken her earlier complaint stopped by. He was solicitous, but as she'd suspected, there wasn't much they could do, given that the note was anonymous and nonthreatening. He cautioned her to be extra careful—which she'd already planned on her own—and to call immediately if even the smallest thing overset her. Then he left.

Shadow suffered a sleepless night, more from fretting over Brent's apparent disinterest than the blasted note.

As usual, he arrived the next morning intent on seeing her to work. She'd tried complaining to him, but he'd insisted it wasn't out of his way, and she enjoyed being with him each day.

He came through the doorway, his green eyes were dark. He was watchful, his gaze piercing, as if he expected something from her, but Shadow had no idea what it was and she was too tired to try to figure it out.

Brent crossed his arms, studying her as she donned her coat. "I don't want you working alone at the shop. Keep Kallie with you when you're there."

For a man with limited interest in her, he was far too autocratic. "It's the holidays," she told him flatly. "She's off three days next week for Thanksgiving and an entire week right before Christmas. Besides that, you can't expect her to spend ten hours a day at the shop."

"Then hire someone else," he insisted. "Hell, if you can't afford it, I'll hire someone."

"You most certainly will not!"

"Shadow." He said her name in two distinct syllables, drawing it out in his exasperation.

"You're being unreasonable," she pointed out. "He hasn't threatened me physically. And maybe we were wrong about your car. Maybe it wasn't him."

"I have a gut feeling about this. It isn't over. I'm sure of it."

Shadow drew a deep breath to steady herself. Then, stiffening her spine, she met his gaze squarely. "It's not really a concern of yours, Brent. You're not responsible for me. I didn't mind at first, because I thought you...well, I thought things would be different between us. But now your folks are in town and here you are, baby-sitting me. I'm a big girl. I can take care of myself."

Brent shoved away from the door in a sudden burst of anger. He ran his fingers through his hair, then gripped a handful and gave a vicious tug. Shadow stared, amazed.

Stomping back to stand directly in front of her, Brent demanded, "Do you do it on purpose?"

"What?" Her eyes were wide, purely fascinated by his spate of ire. She peered up at him, waiting curiously for his answer.

"Drive me nuts! Make me crazy!" His hands came out to grip her shoulders and he gave her a gentle shake. "Make me want you."

That last had been said more softly, almost as if he

hadn't wanted to say it at all. Everything inside Shadow melted. "Brent...you still do? You still want me?"

He stared at her, searching her face as if to reassure himself she could actually be asking such an asinine question, then he released her to give a ferocious growl, throwing his hands up and staring at the ceiling.

"Exactly when," he asked, "have I not been particularly clear about that? *You're* the one who said 'no go,' not me. Hell, I've just been patiently hanging around waiting for you to make up your mind!"

Shadow blinked, then propped her hands on her hips. "How was I supposed to know you were being patient, something I've never seen you be, when it seemed to me you just weren't interested any longer? You haven't once tried to kiss—"

"If I had," he growled, "do you really think I could have left it at that? After touching you, after watching you climax?" He touched her cheek, her jaw. His hand was shaking. "You said you had to have time to think. I've been giving you time."

"But I didn't know that!" she wailed. Then another thought struck her and she frowned suspiciously. "Is that the only reason you seem so concerned about me? You're only trying to—"

"Don't finish that thought." It was the quiet of his voice that filled his words with menace. "I've worried my ass off over you and if you dare to suggest I'd go to these lengths just for a lay...!" He pressed his face close to hers, bending so they were nose-to-nose. "I can have a woman any damn time I want one. It just so happens I want *you*."

He moved away in disgust. "Hell, woman, you've

turned me inside out. All I can do is think about you and...*oof.*"

Shadow threw herself into his arms, literally, giving him only a moment to brace himself for her weight. He stumbled, but immediately steadied himself and wrapped hard arms around her, squeezing her tight. The small telephone table toppled as they bumped into it. He ignored it. "Shadow."

"I have to warn you, Brent," she mumbled against his throat, not willing to loosen her hold on him. "I'm starting to really care about you. I mean, *really* care. I think about you all the time, too. And I miss you when you're not around, and—"

"Hush." His mouth settled on hers, insistent, hot. From one heartbeat to the next, his hands were every-where, touching her breasts, sliding down her back to her bottom, pulling her hard against his body. Just as quickly, he set her away from him.

"Damn." His head was down, his hands on his lean hips. "My parents are at my house waiting for me."

Shadow managed to nod, but it was a difficult feat. "And...and I have to get to the shop."

Brent looked at her, saw the way she gazed back at him, and groaned. "We better get out of here now or we never will."

She nodded again, but she didn't move.

Brent cupped her cheek, his gaze probing. "My par-ents are leaving this evening. Come to dinner with us so I can introduce you."

He wanted her to meet his parents? Her heart thumped in excitement, but she said only, "I'd love to."

Brent stared down at her, then his gaze dropped to her shirt. It was pale blue, with two cuddly stuffed bears printed on the front, one over each breast. Below was written *Don't You Just Love my Teddies?* He said, "Uh, Shadow?"

"Hmm?"

"Before dinner? Do you think you could cover your teddies?"

A slow grin came to her lips. "Are you afraid I'll wear something that would embarrass you in front of your mama?"

"You? Of course not." His arms circled her waist. "You're always dressed in the height of fashion."

Shadow punched him lightly in the ribs. "Tell me where we'll be eating and I'll dress appropriately."

Brent pretended to give the matter serious thought, then said, "Wear something black. That should cover it and satisfy my mother."

"I'm not particularly concerned with satisfying your mother." She touched his bottom lip. "Will it satisfy you?"

He gave her a sinner's wicked smile. "I have no doubt you'll satisfy me, honey. That's why I've been going crazy."

Feeling her stomach tumble with the meaning of his words, Shadow decided she'd better behave—for her own salvation. Otherwise, she just might drag him to the bedroom and take him forcibly, her work and his parents be damned. Since she couldn't be positive he would appreciate her effort, she bent to right the telephone table that had overturned.

Brent was at her side, helping. "I hope nothing broke."

"Just scattered a few things. Don't worry about it. It was worth any mess to see your fit of temper."

"I don't indulge in fits of temper. What you saw was my remarkable restraint in keeping my hands off you."

Shadow laughed, but the humor instantly died when Brent picked up the note. He glanced at her still face, then read.

His expression hardened with annoyance. "You weren't going to tell me about this?"

"Actually...no. I was planning on throwing it away."

"Throw it away? Some maniac writes you a threatening note and you don't intend to tell me?"

Shadow frowned. "It wasn't exactly threatening."

"I beg your pardon. The exact wording is, 'I see you all the time. Soon you'll see me, too.'"

Shadow blinked, then frowned. "Let me see that." After Brent handed her the note, she quickly skimmed it, then raised worried eyes to his face. "It's another one. He must have dropped it though the mail slot last night, after I'd gone to bed."

"You mean this is the second note?"

Nodding, Shadow said, "I already spoke to the police, so you can quit frowning at me."

That didn't appease him. "What exactly did the first note say?"

Shadow recited it as best she could remember. "He evidently slipped both notes through my mail slot. The other one was here when I got in yesterday."

"Then this one," he said, "was delivered during the night while you were asleep."

Shadow couldn't help it. She paled at the thought of a man creeping around her house during the night.

Brent took her arm and started out the front door, making certain it was locked behind them. He hustled her along to her car, barely letting her feet touch the ground. She could feel the tension in him, his annoyance. "I've had enough, Shadow. I'm going to have an alarm system installed today. No! Not a word out of you."

She stopped in the middle of the sidewalk. "You'll get more than a word from me if you don't stop being such a jerk."

"I'm a worried jerk, all right?" She didn't answer and he sighed. He reached out, caught her hand and pulled her alongside him. "I'm sorry. I'm not used to worrying."

"Then stop doing it."

"I also don't want you at the shop alone, or anywhere else alone, for that matter."

Shadow could only shake her head. "I'm a single woman, Brent. I *live* alone. Or are you planning to move in?" She could tell by the look on his face that he wasn't, that she had presented him with something of a quandary.

Collecting himself, Brent said easily, "Once the alarm is installed, you should be safe enough." He stopped beside her car and looked at her with a frown. "That is, if you're not afraid?"

Shadow withered him with a look of disdain. "I'm not afraid of the dark or bogeymen or rainstorms." Her lie sounded credible even to her own ears. She was afraid, but he didn't need to know it. "I think you're right about an alarm system, though."

"Of course I am." He looked relieved at her concurrence.

"However," she added sternly, "I'll be the one to have the alarm installed. I'm not penniless. And it is my house and my hide that'll be protected. So it's my responsibility."

Brent said only, "At least let me put in the order. I want to make certain you get an infallible system." When she started to object, he added, "You can't cut corners on this sort of thing. It should cover the perimeter of the house, and most especially the doors and all the windows...."

"I agree."

He smiled, satisfied. "I'll talk to the security people today." He gave her a brief, hard kiss, then took her keys to unlock her car, seeing her safely deposited inside. "I have an early meeting to get out of the way so I can spend the rest of the afternoon with my parents. I'll follow you to work, then come by later for you tonight. We'll go to dinner just as soon as you've had time to change. All right?"

"If I say yes, do I get another kiss?" His eyes darkened further and it fascinated Shadow. Seeing his gaze settle on her mouth, she tipped her face up to him, her lips slightly pursed. Brent swore softly, then cupped her cheeks, now cold from the frigid winter air, and took her mouth.

She wouldn't need her heater if he kept that up. She slumped in the seat when he drew away, patted her cheek, then locked her door and closed it. "Drive carefully," he called from the window, and left for his own car.

Shadow stared after him. She wasn't at all certain she approved of his bossiness, but she more than approved of his kisses. Maybe she could get him to compromise on the rest. And as for her not staying alone at the shop, she hadn't really agreed to that, but she also hadn't wanted to argue with him about it.

But then, on second thought, arguing with Brent was probably the second most exciting thing she'd ever done with him. All in all, he kept her senses stimulated. She couldn't wait to see him that night.

THEY HAD THEIR FIRST huge argument the minute they got back to her house. Shadow started down her front walk, and Brent knew he couldn't hesitate any longer. "Just a minute, Shadow."

She glanced at him with a smile. Well, her smile wouldn't last much longer, but hopefully she'd understand. He didn't, but then, around Shadow, he never seemed to understand himself. He crossed his arms over his chest, ignored the howling wind and said, "I have to tell you the code for the alarm system."

Her smile never slipped. "Alarm system?"

"The one I had installed today."

She caught her hair back from her face, gave him a quizzical look and said, as if speaking to a simpleton, "I haven't chosen an alarm system yet, therefore it's impossible that one has been installed."

He'd done what was right, damn it, and he'd just keep telling himself that. "I had it installed. All the downstairs doors and windows are covered. Security lights will be taken care of tomorrow morning." He drew a breath, eyed her still features and continued. "If anyone tries to break in, the lights will come on and the police will automatically be called."

She glanced over her shoulder at the house. "You did this?"

"I want you safe," he said reasonably.

When she faced him again, her expression was no longer still. "No, you want to take charge of my life," she accused, and he couldn't very well deny it. When he remained quiet, she threw up her arms and shouted, "Good grief, one stalker is enough."

She turned to stomp away, slipped on the ice and started to fall. Brent had already been reaching for her, and he grabbed for her waist, but wasn't quick enough. They both went down, him flat on his back, Shadow draped across him.

Her knee damn near got him in the groin when she immediately struggled to sit up. He held her tightly. "Why is it," he asked, leashing his temper with care, "that every damn time I'm near you, you bring me low."

She whipped around, fully atop him, and said not two inches away from his face, "You keep overstepping yourself, that's why! I won't have it, Brent."

Thinking quickly, he suggested, "You can pay me back. It's an excellent system and now it's done and you know it was necessary."

"It was my decision to make!"

He'd never known a woman like her. Every other woman of his acquaintance wanted to be taken care of, wanted him to spend his money—the more the better. They'd have been flattered with his concern, complimented by his thoughtfulness, but not Shadow. No, she looked ready to bang his head into the icy sidewalk.

Being a perverse bastard, he smiled. "I'm sorry."

Shadow drew back, watching him warily. "You don't look sorry. You're grinning like a sinner."

"That's because you're so cute. No," he said, catching her when she would have flung away from him again, "I'm not patronizing you. You are cute and I like you and I worry about you, whether you want me to— hell, whether I want me to—and so I did it and I'm sorry it upset you, but I'd do it again in order to keep you safe."

She stared at him a moment longer, then grumbled, "You're impossible. Let me up. I hurt my hip when I fell."

He was immediately concerned. His own posterior felt bruised, as well as frozen. Three times. Three times now he'd ended up on his back in front of her. He caught her beneath the arms and lifted them both together. Dusting snowflakes and ice crystals from her coat, he asked, "Do you need me to carry you?"

Her look nearly fried him, despite the temperature. "How do I get in?"

Brent chose to take her question as a good sign. As if she hadn't just been glaring at him, he put his arm around her shoulders and started her forward. "I'll show you."

He produced a new key for her—to go with the new lock—and then punched in the code on the keypad. "Always do it right away or the police will come knocking to see what's wrong."

Looking around her house as if it wasn't her own anymore, she asked, "How much do I owe you?"

Brent winced, divided the actual price in half and watched her face for signs of distress. He really had no idea of her finances, though she claimed to be comfortable enough.

She never blinked. She just went to her checkbook and made out a check. As she handed it to him, she said, "I'll forgive you this once. Just this once. On the condition you promise to never ever again—"

"I promise," he said, not even wanting her to finish that statement. He had no idea what he might do in the future, so it was best to keep his promise vague.

She didn't look at all convinced, but said only, "I

have to go shower. I'll be back down in fifteen minutes.''

"We have time," he told her, hoping the shower would restore her good mood. He loved her smiles, her quick laughter, the way she found humor in everything.

When she emerged twenty minutes later, already wearing a black cloak, her dark curls decorated with a silk ribbon, Brent was relieved to see her smiling.

She flitted around her house, talking nonstop, apparently excited about the evening. As she pulled on a pair of black leather gloves, Brent gave a brief thought to his parents. His father was amiable enough, but his mother could be extremely rigid to the women Brent chose to date. Of course, Shadow was different, and since his mother wasn't stupid, he imagined she'd quickly realize that Shadow was open and honest. He only hoped she didn't hurt Shadow's feelings or in some way insult her.

Brent held her hand on the drive, listening to her light conversation on everything from the sales at the shop to how her backside was still slightly numb from her fall. He couldn't recall this much enjoyment from chitchatting with any other woman. But Shadow was so lively, always smiling, quick to forgive—thankfully—and just as quick to laugh. She enjoyed life, even the mundane ventures, and that made him enjoy them, too.

"You didn't bruise yourself, did you?"

Her eyes twinkled at him in the dim interior of his car. "I didn't look, actually, so I don't know." She added, peering at him through her lashes, "But I wouldn't be a bit surprised."

"Should I kiss it for you to make it all better?"

"That could work," she murmured with false sincerity, only to say, "but a massage would probably be more effective. If you really want to help, that is."

The thought of getting his hands on her soft, rounded bottom again played havoc with his libido. It had been too long since he'd really touched her and it seemed he'd been wanting her forever.

His eyes shone at her, intent and filled with subtle meaning. "Depend on it."

A valet parked the car, and after Shadow had taken Brent's arm, they started inside.

He watched her expression, curious as to how she would react to the grand and elegant establishment. It was new, and Brent thought it particularly ostentatious, but his father had chosen it. Usually his parents' company could be excessively boring, especially in "polite" society. They were nearly regimented in their manners and social behavior. He had looked upon Shadow's company as a salvation to the evening. But now he began to worry.

He didn't know if Shadow would be comfortable in the outlandishly expensive surroundings. Not for the world would Brent want to make her ill at ease. He adored her forthright and outspoken manner, and wanted to encourage it. He wanted Shadow to be herself, always, despite his parents' opinions or the quiet elegance of the dining room. He totally disregarded the fact that up until meeting Shadow, he himself had been very remote and reserved.

She didn't gaze around in wonder at the glittering chandeliers hanging overhead, and the uniformed checker who asked for her cloak only received a dimpled smile and a simple thank-you. All would be fine,

Brent decided; he'd worried for nothing. Shadow could definitely take care of herself.

She took off her cloak—and he got his first good look at what she wore.

5

THE LOUD BURST of laughter was startling. Peering over her shoulder, her expression deliberately demure, Shadow asked, "Is something wrong?"

Brent grinned at her, then kissed her fingers. "You never disappoint me, sweetheart, do you know that?"

She bestowed a very pleased smile on him. "I do try to be accommodating."

Dismissing the curious and disapproving stares, Brent took Shadow's arm as they made their way to the table. She looked delectable. And she had followed his suggestion—at least as far as the black was concerned. "The suspenders add a certain sensuality to the outfit."

She didn't slow her pace. "Do you think so?"

"Umm. You look like a very sexy schoolgirl."

She slanted him a provocative look. "I keep telling you—sexy comes in many different forms."

"I think I like your form just fine." And her "form" was clearly defined in the narrow velvet slacks. They were high waisted, cinching tight just below her breasts, lying smooth over her belly. Wide suspenders went over her shoulders and then crisscrossed in the back. Her white silk blouse buttoned with pearls and her pointed collar closed about her throat with a thin, black silk tie, as expertly knotted as Brent's own.

The outfit emphasized the lush fullness of her breasts. The material of the blouse was so soft and clinging Brent could detect each swell and curve. He wondered if she could possibly be wearing a bra. He couldn't see the outlines of it, but neither could he see even a hint of her nipples, and God knows he looked.

He felt his body reacting to his thoughts, and brought his attention back to his waiting parents. They were wide-eyed as Brent and Shadow approached. Slowly, his father stood, while his mother only laid a hand to her throat, clearly shocked. Brent made the introductions, doing his best to hold in his laughter.

"How do you do, Mr. Bramwell?"

Brent watched, smiling, as Shadow thrust her hand out to his father, taking him off guard.

With only a moment's hesitation, his father took her proffered hand. "Martin, please. It's nice to meet you, er, Shadow, was it?"

"Yes, sir. Shadow Callahan." At his curious look, she expounded, "My parents had a whimsical way about them. I have two younger sisters, Storm and Windy, and a baby brother, Sunny—with a *u*."

Brent was amazed he'd never heard this story. "Did she name each of you according to the weather when you were born?"

Shadow sent him a crooked smile. "No. Actually, it was the weather when we were conceived, or so I'm told."

Shadow was seated across from Brent's mother, and when she gasped, Shadow looked up in concern. "Are you all right? Did you choke on your drink?"

Brent reached over to pat his mother's back, handing her the water goblet. "Here, Mother. Sip this." Then he dismissed her, smiling gently at Shadow.

The waiter appeared, taking orders for their drinks.

Martin said, "I'll have another Scotch. And a white wine for Debra." He turned to Brent. "Scotch?"

Nodding, Brent said, "That'll be fine." All eyes turned to Shadow.

"No alcohol for me, please. How about a soda?"

The waiter, without flicking an eyelash, walked away. But Debra frowned at her. "That was rather crudely put, young lady. Do you have difficulty maintaining a discreet consumption?"

Shadow smiled with tender remembrance, forewarning Brent of disaster. "Not at all. At least, I don't think so." Then she dropped her bomb. "But Brent got me a little drunk the other day, and took complete advantage of the situation. I don't intend to give him such an opportunity again."

This time it was Brent who choked, while his parents stared. Damn the little witch, she was probably getting even over the alarm system.

In a performance worthy of the stage, Shadow seemed to rethink her words. "Oh, I don't mean...that is, he was a complete gentleman. Too much so, in fact, which was actually the problem."

"Shadow..." he said in warning.

Of course she ignored him.

Patting his hand as if to placate him, she said, "You know, Brent has a terrible time controlling his temper. He's just too intense for things to ever go smoothly around him." She leaned forward slightly to confide, "It's one of the things I like most about him."

Martin blinked at her, then slowly grinned. "Is that so? I've always found my son to be in perfect control of every situation. He must always be the employer, not the employee."

"I know just what you mean. He tries to bulldoze

me, too. The stories I could tell..." Brent turned his hand over and squeezed her fingers. "Well," she said, giving him a look, "maybe that's for another time. But I can hold my own. Not even Brent, gorgeous and appealing as he is, can run my life for me."

This time she looked directly at him, ignoring his parents. "I have things well in hand."

The drinks came, keeping Brent from saying anything in return. No sooner had the waiter taken the order for their meals and departed than Debra again tried to grab her own measure of control over the dinner conversation.

"Brent, Joan sends her love. She misses you fiercely."

Brent shook his head, casting a surreptitious look at Shadow. "She misses my money, Mother, not me."

"You're being uncharitable. Of course she expected you to show a certain amount of affection with gifts and such. That's the way of it." Debra shrugged delicately, expressing her unconcern.

Shadow asked, "Is this the past fiancée who is making a pest of herself?"

Brent nodded, watching Shadow for some sign of jealousy. There was none and it annoyed him. "She no doubt expected to see me over Thanksgiving," he told Shadow, egging her on just a bit.

Debra continued to address Shadow, undaunted. "Brent gave her a beautiful diamond bracelet just before they broke off. She still wears it, poor girl."

"He's generous to a fault," Shadow agreed, her expression impossible to read. "Just today, he tried to buy me this expensive security alarm system." She sighed dramatically. "But I persevere. Hopefully, he'll catch on soon that I'm not a charity case and I don't want his money." She grinned. "But I do enjoy arguing with him. He's so outrageous."

Martin laughed, while Debra looked very disapproving. Brent simply sat back and enjoyed himself. Never before had he seen anyone put his mother in her place, and Shadow did it with ease.

Dinner was certainly different, Brent decided. The food was excellent, of course, but the conversation surrounding the table was a volley of subtle insults from his mother, each of which Shadow deflected with quick wit and candid honesty. Brent realized with some surprise that his father was equally amused, and they shared an indulgent masculine chuckle.

Shadow ate with perfect manners, but unlike most women of Brent's acquaintance, she had a hearty appetite, and no fear of displaying it. He and his parents had chosen seafood, but Shadow had ordered steak and potatoes.

After she'd eaten every bite, she leaned back in her seat, patted her belly and sighed. "That was delicious. My stomach was growling all the way over here."

Debra was appalled. "You have a very bad habit of speaking thoughts that are better left private."

In a mock-mournful voice, Shadow answered, "I know. I have a lot of nasty habits. Most people do, however. What bad habits do you have?"

Debra frowned at her. "I have no idea."

Shadow's grin could be called nothing less than sly, but her tone was pleasant enough. "Would you like for me to help you distinguish a few of them?"

"Well! I never."

Brows raised, she said, "You should," then added when everyone grew quiet, "No really. I've always believed we should be aware of ourselves and our shortcomings, just as we should acknowledge our accomplishments and our more favorable characteristics. It's good to know yourself inside and out. That way, no one can take you by surprise with an insult, because you'll already be aware of it—" she tilted her head "—or else know it to be mere malice or spite that provoked them to lie."

Brent studied her, intrigued anew. She'd said that a lot of people thought her nutty, and he had issued that damn insult as well. He wondered now just how much guff she'd had to put up with from the conformists. His heart swelled with compassion. "All that?" he asked gently. "I had no idea." He reached over to take her hand, unmindful of the attention he received from his parents. "What would you say your own faults are?"

He didn't mean for her to be overly serious, to lay herself open to criticism from himself and his parents. He'd only hoped to tease her into another smile. But Shadow took his question to heart. "I'm too trusting. And not very perceptive when it comes to innuendo or discreet insults." She grinned at Brent's mother. "Your insults were thankfully plain. But there have been others who thought it was fun to make a fool of me." She shrugged. "I guess I'm an easy mark."

"That's very hard to imagine," Brent murmured. "You're too smart for that."

"Smart," she agreed without modesty, "but I also have a very strange perception of people and their place around me. I find humor in almost everything, even when it doesn't exist. It made it rough getting through school, because everyone seemed to think I was slow or simple, even though I made high grades and was on the dean's list in college. Also, as your mama already noted, I'm entirely too candid."

Brent felt tenderness expand inside him. Squeezing her hand, he commented, "But you're certainly a snappy dresser."

Shadow laughed. "I like to think so."

There was a heavy pause at the table, then Debra tossed down her napkin. "Will you have any time off for Christmas?"

Shadow looked at her curiously. "I'll close Christmas Eve and Christmas Day."

Debra turned to Brent. "Get her to take some time off so you can bring her home for Christmas." She gave her attention to folding her napkin as she added, "Your grandparents would enjoy meeting her, I'm sure. And it would probably end Joan's pursuit if she saw you with Shadow."

Enthusiastic about the proposal, Martin said, "That's an excellent idea! We'd be pleased to have you join us, Shadow. Very pleased."

Amazed by his parents' acceptance, Brent heard Shadow say, "Thank you. I'll see what *I* can work out." Which Brent knew meant she didn't want or need his interference. He bit back a grin. Her independence was refreshing, even when it annoyed him.

Brent spent the entire drive to the airport pondering the amazing means Shadow had used to win over his mother: simple honesty. During their farewells, Debra actually told Brent how lucky he was to have found such a levelheaded female. Martin, winking at Shadow, said, "And she's very cute besides."

Brent thought Shadow to be a bit more than "cute," and plans for the coming night had him ending the send-off with noticeable haste. His parents smiled after him as he turned away, Shadow by his side.

"Brent, you're being unbelievably conspicuous."

Without slowing his pace to the car, Brent asked, "About what?"

"About wanting to sleep with me."

They were in the parking lot, the night air too brisk, but the wind thankfully calm for once. He stopped and turned to stare down at her. The glow of a full moon highlighted her soft black curls, her pale cheeks, her wide dark eyes. Brent felt nearly overwhelmed with a myriad of sensations and he didn't fully understand a one of them. Except for the need that was both recognizable and unique. Lust, but stronger than lust. He wanted her, right now, this instant. He wanted to be inside her, hearing her cries, feeling the clench of her body around his erection as he went deep, so deep she became a part of him.

Searching her face, he noted when her lips parted slightly, when her breathing sped up, and he bent to touch her mouth with his own, a light, brief touch.

"It's true," he said into her mouth, inhaling her scent and the cold crisp evening air. "I want you so much I hurt, sweetheart. More than I can recall ever wanting anything." She trembled and Brent cupped her cheeks gently with his gloved hands. "I'm also willing to wait if you're not ready. I want you to want me, too. I want you to want me as much."

"I do."

Her warm breath fogged in the darkness between them. Brent groaned and took her hand again, nearly running to his car.

They were almost to her house when Shadow suddenly broke the silence, whispering, "Brent? It's been a long time for me."

He parked the car, then turned to Shadow, seeing the glimmer in her eyes, so huge and filled with anxiety and urgency. He said softly, "You think I'm going to drag you inside and straight to your bedroom? Maybe pounce on you?"

"I don't know."

Always so honest, he thought, and laughed softly. "I could probably manage ten minutes of conversation, if that'd help."

An impish grin, only slightly nervous, flashed across her face. "Are you going to be timing it?"

"Very discreetly. You won't notice me watching the clock, I promise."

"All right." She bit her lip, but asked, "Maybe we could warm up a bit with a few more of those kisses?"

"Oh, there'll be kisses." His muscles tensed with that statement. He'd driven to her home with an erection, with shaking hands, and part of that was due to thinking of all the places, all the ways, he intended to kiss her. "Plenty of kisses, Shadow. Don't worry about that."

Once inside the house, Brent reset the alarm code, then deliberately led Shadow to the family room. He needed time to collect himself and garner his patience. She didn't deserve to be rushed, and he wanted her too much to test himself. Shadow watched him with attentive wariness.

Attempting a casualness he didn't feel, Brent asked, "Would you mind if I lit the fire?"

She shook her head. "Everything is ready. There should be some matches on the mantel. I try to keep things set up so..."

"Shadow." He said her name softly, hoping to reassure her, to help her relax. "I'm not going to jump on you. I promise."

"And here I was so hopeful," she teased, more to herself than anything.

"That's better." Brent had a warm, blazing fire going in no time. Keeping his gaze off Shadow with an effort, he went around turning off the lamps she had just turned on. When he stopped before her, he said, "That's much nicer, don't you think?"

"Yes." And then she came to her feet. "Would you like something to drink?"

Brent smiled at her lazily. "Do you have any wine?"

"No!" She gave him a dirty look for that. "But I do have some eggnog, and some lemon snap cookies I bought from this little bakery that does them especially well. They always save an extra batch for me at the end of the day. I have a running account. I just grab them from the back room on my way home—"

Her rambling monologue stopped abruptly. She gulped.

"All right." Brent didn't want her tense. He wanted her hot, soft. He smiled, but it was a painful smile. "We'll drink the eggnog and eat the cookies. But don't forget, I'm watching the clock."

They went to the kitchen together. Shadow bustled around, filling their glasses and picking up a good half dozen cookies to put on a plate. Brent was proud of his show of indulgence. Waiting until they had reseated themselves on the sofa and Shadow had stuffed an entire cookie into her mouth, Brent asked, "How long has it been for you, Shadow?"

Still chewing, she raised her brows in question, so he clarified. "How long since you've been with a man?"

She didn't choke, she didn't gasp with indignation or look insulted. She shrugged slightly, then swallowed. "Awhile."

"How long is awhile?"

With a look that was almost apologetic, she said, "Seven years?"

"*Seven...*" Brent stared at her, thoroughly appalled, and Shadow downed another cookie. That made three for her. He himself hadn't touched the things. "Are you telling me you haven't had sex in seven years?"

Again she had to chew and swallow before she could say, "Don't sound so disbelieving. I told you I'd had terrible luck with men. After my husband, and before I was engaged the second time, I had a few semiserious relationships. They were total fiascoes. I ended up looking like a fool. So I swore off men."

Damn if his heart didn't expand. He could actually feel it, crowding his chest. "Then you saw me."

"Just one look, as the song goes." Her admission had the effect of gasoline on an already raging inferno.

Brent leaned toward her. He studied her soft mouth, now dusty with cookie crumbs, her narrow nose and her stubborn chin and her incredible eyes. "I haven't been able to put you from my mind since that first look."

Shadow blindly reached for another cookie.

"Are the cookies really that good?" Amusement warred with impatience.

Shadow looked at the cookie in her hand. "Uh...I have no idea. I don't think I've tasted a single one." She turned her gaze up to him, her honeyed eyes very sincere and warm. "I always eat when I'm nervous. I'm sorry. Really."

Brent very gently disengaged the cookie from her hand, placing it back on the plate. "Come here, honey. Let me just hold you for a bit."

She did. Then she whispered, "I know I'm acting like an idiot, but I want things to be right with you, Brent."

Because things for her usually went wrong, where men were concerned? He shook his head. "Hush."

This time it would be different, because he was different. He'd see to it that she enjoyed herself. A lot.

He'd slipped his suit coat off before he made the fire, and now she snuggled close, pressing her nose into his chest and breathing deeply.

Sifting his fingers through her hair, he dislodged her ribbon, then laid it on the coffee table with the cookies. With a crooked finger under her chin, he tilted her face up and kissed her.

She immediately softened against him, relaxed, and he realized he should have kissed her sooner. He licked her lips, teasing and tasting, sliding deep inside, stroking her with his tongue as he'd soon be stroking her body. His erection throbbed and he knew he was going too fast. He pulled back, lightly nipping her throat, her ear.

"I love it when you kiss me."

Her words were breathless, hot. Brent intended to show her all the other pleasurable places he would kiss her. *Control,* he reminded himself. This first time had to be just right. And knowing Shadow, the best way to control the situation would be to let her think *she* had the control.

At one time that thought might have been unacceptable; with Shadow, it made his lust more urgent than ever.

Slowly, Brent began to lean back on the sofa. Following his lead, Shadow ended up sprawled over his chest, her slight weight pressing into him. With each deep breath, her stiffened nipples caressed him. Her arms were tight, her legs restless. Brent couldn't stop the groan from deep in his throat.

Shadow didn't seem to notice his hands on her hips, aligning her pelvis with his own. She didn't notice the way he slid one leg between hers, opening her to his touch, having her practically ride his thigh. She did pay attention, however, when he began unknotting her tie.

"Brent?"

He kissed her bottom lip, tugged gently on it with his teeth. "You could do the same for me."

"All right." Between their fumbling hands, they soon had their collars open. Brent had quite a few more buttons undone on Shadow's shirt than she had managed to undo on his. He stared at the smooth, creamy rise of her breasts beneath the shirt.

"You didn't wear a bra. I couldn't be sure at dinner."

"I wore a teddy."

Amused, he asked, "You wore a teddy? I thought you preferred fun stuff to the traditional. Teddies are pretty damn traditional."

"No." She curled a finger in the hair on his chest, not quite meeting his gaze. "I said other things can be equally as sexy. But a good teddy has its place."

Brent traced his fingertips along the opening of her shirt, touching satin and lace and warm soft skin. He undid a few more buttons, then pushed her suspenders and the shirt off her shoulders.

"You are so damn beautiful," he murmured, so close to the edge he didn't know if he could hang on much longer. This kiss was different, filled with hunger and possession. He worked the shirt from her body, leaving her back bare to his hands, her throat and upper chest available to his mouth. He nuzzled against her, his lips rooting over her satin-covered breasts until he found a nipple. It was a gentle bite, but Shadow jumped, then groaned when he began to suckle. Her back arched and her belly pressed down, inadvertently stroking his hard-on.

In a rasping voice, he said, "Let's get out of these clothes."

Shadow moved, dazed, to Brent's side. She lay there, eyes wide and soft, while he pulled away her shoes and unfastened her trousers. Slowly, teasing himself, he dragged them off her hips and down the length of her legs. He felt so urgent, so hungry, he couldn't take his gaze off her as he stood to jerk free of his own clothes. The teddy was mere decoration, in no way concealing her breasts with the rosy, puckered nipples, or the dark triangle of hair between her thighs.

His chest rose and fell with his uneven breathing.

And then she said, "I gather my ten minutes are up?"

SHADOW SAW BRENT GO STILL, but only for a moment. Beautifully naked except for a pair of charcoal-gray, snug-fitting boxers that barely contained his erection, he awed her. She wanted to touch him, to explore his sex with her hands, but he seemed on the ragged edge as he came to kneel before her. His large hands settled lightly on her thighs. "Don't be shy, sweetheart. Not with me."

"No. No, I'm not." He was so large and imposing, the width of his muscled chest blocking her view of the fire, which framed his body with a golden glow. "I want to see you," she admitted.

His smile was heart-meltingly sensual. The warmth of his palms penetrated the skimpy teddy, and Shadow

Play the
"LAS VEGAS" Game
and get
3 FREE GIFTS!

FREE GIFTS!

FREE GIFTS!

1. Pull back all 3 tabs on the card at right. Then check the claim chart to see what we have for you — 2 FREE BOOKS and a gift — ALL YOURS! ALL FREE!

2. Send back this card and you'll receive brand-new Harlequin Temptation® novels. These books have a cover price of $3.99 each in the U.S. and $4.50 each in Canada, but they are yours to keep absolutely free.

3. There's no catch. You're under no obligation to buy anything. We charge nothing — ZERO — for your first shipment. And you don't have to make any minimum number of purchases — not even one!

4. The fact is, thousands of readers enjoy receiving their books by mail from the Harlequin Reader Service®. They enjoy the convenience of home delivery...they like getting the best new novels at discount prices, BEFORE they're available in stores...and they love their *Heart to Heart* newsletter featuring author news, horoscopes, recipes, book reviews and much more!

5. We hope that after receiving your free books you'll want to remain a subscriber. But the choice is yours — to continue or cancel, any time at all! So why not take us up on our invitation, with no risk of any kind. You'll be glad you did!

© 1998 HARLEQUIN ENTERPRISES LTD.

® and ™ are trademarks owned by Harlequin Enterprises Ltd.

Visit us online at
www.eHarlequin.com

FREE!
No Obligation to Buy!
No Purchase Necessary!

Play the

"LAS VEGAS"

Game

PEEL BACK HERE ▶
PEEL BACK HERE ▶
PEEL BACK HERE ▶

YES! I have pulled back the 3 tabs. Please send me all the free Harlequin Temptation® books and the gift for which I qualify. I understand that I am under no obligation to purchase any books, as explained on the back and opposite page.

342 HDL DC4W

142 HDL DC4N
(H-T-OS-05/01)

NAME   (PLEASE PRINT CLEARLY)

ADDRESS

APT.#   CITY

STATE/PROV.   ZIP/POSTAL CODE

7	7	7	**GET 2 FREE BOOKS & A FREE MYSTERY GIFT!**
🍀	🍀	🍀	**GET 2 FREE BOOKS!**
🍒	🍒	🍒	**GET 1 FREE BOOK!**
🔔	🔔	🔔	**TRY AGAIN!**

Offer limited to one per household and not valid to current Harlequin Temptation® subscribers. All orders subject to approval.

▼ DETACH AND MAIL TODAY ▼

The Harlequin Reader Service®—Here's how it works:

Accepting your 2 free books and gift places you under no obligation to buy anything. You may keep the books and gift and return the shipping statement marked "cancel." If you do not cancel, about a month later we'll send you 4 additional novels and bill you just $3.34 each in the U.S., or $3.80 each in Canada, plus 25¢ shipping & handling per book and applicable taxes if any.* That's the complete price and — compared to cover prices of $3.99 each in the U.S. and $4.50 each in Canada — it's quite a bargain! You may cancel at any time, but if you choose to continue, every month we'll send you 4 more books, which you may either purchase at the discount price or return to us and cancel your subscription.

*Terms and prices subject to change without notice. Sales tax applicable in N.Y. Canadian residents will be charged applicable provincial taxes and GST.

If offer card is missing write to: Harlequin Reader Service, 3010 Walden Ave., P.O. Box 1867, Buffalo, NY 14240-1867

BUSINESS REPLY MAIL
FIRST-CLASS MAIL   PERMIT NO. 717   BUFFALO, NY

POSTAGE WILL BE PAID BY ADDRESSEE

HARLEQUIN READER SERVICE
3010 WALDEN AVE
PO BOX 1867
BUFFALO NY 14240-9952

NO POSTAGE
NECESSARY
IF MAILED
IN THE
UNITED STATES

closed her eyes in pleasure as he caressed her hips, down her thighs, over the arches of her feet. Keeping her eyes closed, she grinned.

"You're ticklish," he observed with rough-toned affection.

"A little." Her nipples drew tighter, and between her thighs she ached. She needed him.

Brent pressed his face into her belly and his arms went around her to hold her tight. It was an endearing embrace, filling Shadow with warmth. Moved by his tenderness, she tangled her fingers in his hair, holding him close.

Any concerns or trepidation she had been harboring evaporated. The things Brent made her feel were too complex to understand or control. Later she would try to figure them out, but for now, she only wanted to experience them fully.

"Tell me what you feel," he said as he stroked her breasts through the teddy. Her breath sighed out; her body trembled. He alternately watched her face and his hands on her body.

He grasped her hips and pulled her to the edge of the sofa, snug against his groin. There was only the insubstantial material of the teddy to shield her, and she was aware of every throbbing inch of his erection.

"You have large hands," she noted as his palms stroked her from breasts to thighs, covering nearly every inch of her body.

"Yes, thankfully. I can't decide where to kiss you first." He lowered the straps of the teddy, baring her breasts. "Tell me what you're feeling," he said again, then caught her nipples between his fingers, lightly pinching and tugging, rolling her sensitized flesh until Shadow found it impossible to remain still.

"Desperate," she said in a low murmur, "I feel tight and urgent and almost in pain. Brent, please..." She ended with a groan.

He leaned forward to lave her with his tongue. "I've waited forever for you, Shadow. You have to give me time to play."

She held him to her as he sucked strongly at her breast. The tension in her built and drew tighter, stronger, until she moaned, feeling on the verge of climax. As if he knew, understood, his hand slid over her belly, then lower, between her thighs, where she was open and wanting.

His fingers were insistent, knowing. The material covering her grew damp as his middle fingertip found one ultrasensitive spot, pressing, plying.

She squeezed her eyes shut, dropped her head back on the sofa. Brent switched to her other breast, and even the warmth of the air caressing her bare nipple, now wet from his mouth, was a stimulant. As if he'd read her mind, he released her breast and blew gently on the straining peak, watching avidly as it puckered further, as Shadow cried out, her hips thrusting against his fingers.

Brent reached for the snaps at the seam of her teddy, no longer willing or able to wait and tease. With no warning at all, he pressed two fingers deep inside her. She cried out, shocked, alarmed by the slight discomfort, and so close to coming she couldn't seem to see straight. Everything blurred, spun. "Brent!"

He ignored her, his fingers sliding in and out in a tantalizing rhythm, unhindered by the tight clasp of her body. He simply forced his way in, then withdrew, again and again.

"Oh...oh..." She literally felt faint, her heart beating far too fast.

Brent lowered himself, his mouth urgently burning a trail from her breasts to her open legs. He bit the soft flesh on the inside of her right thigh, and then he was there, his mouth covering her, his rough tongue licking, sucking.

Shadow fell apart. She'd never experienced anything like it, mind numbing and burning, a pleasure so sharp she felt herself fracture. He held her there, pushing her, not letting the pleasure fade until she went limp and boneless. Her heart was still pounding too hard, a deafening tattoo in her ears. Her skin prickled, both with sweat and sensation.

As if from far away, she felt Brent's tender touch, the stroking of his knuckles across her cheek, the sweep of his hand over her hair. "Hey, sleepyhead." His voice was amused, concerned. "Have I put you out for the night?"

She struggled to open her eyes, but it was an effort. He smiled down at her, his green eyes tender, still hot with arousal. "Brent..." His name sounded slurred, nearly incoherent. She didn't understand what was wrong. "I'm so sorry, but I'm..." She couldn't quite fashion the right words to explain. Exhaustion pulled at her; she was more tired than she could ever remember being in her entire life. She gave up and closed her eyes again. "I am sorry."

She barely heard Brent's disbelieving laugh. Mumbling under his breath, he said, "I should market myself as a sleep aid."

It was beyond Shadow to reply, though she wanted to. She wanted to sit up and look at him and explore his splendid body and kiss him as he'd kissed her. She couldn't. It was all she could do to blink at him again, to bring his handsome face into focus.

There was a resigned sigh, a gust of breath that gently blew her hair, and then she felt Brent's strong arms slide beneath her. "To bed with you, sleepyhead. I suppose my turn will come in the morning."

She wanted to protest, to tell him that it wasn't fair he'd have to wait. Something was terribly wrong, but what? He laid her in the bed and she managed to whisper again, "I'm sorry."

He kissed her forehead. "You obviously work too damn hard."

But that wasn't it, she knew, yet she couldn't quite get the thoughts to form in her mind. All she could comprehend was her embarrassment and her disappointment.

"Brent..."

"Go on to sleep," he said, "and if you wake up refreshed, I'll be here."

Shadow forced her heavy eyes open to stare up at him. She whispered miserably, "I told you I had wretched luck with men. Now you see what I mean."

"Nonsense. You have me." To her blurry mind, he sounded agitated, but not angry. "I'd say you have excellent luck." He stood next to the bed, skimmed off his boxers, then stretched.

Shadow looked at him, seeing him through a gray haze. His erection drew her attention first and she groaned, but the sound was too weak, too faint for him to notice. His legs were long and strong, his stomach flat and lightly muscled, not nearly as hairy as his chest, and very appealing. Broad, straight shoulders and lean, sinewy arms... He was beautiful and Shadow was beginning to wonder if she'd ever get to fully enjoy his body.

"Don't look so glum, sweetheart. I'm almost certain I'll survive." He slid into bed beside her, pulling her close and settling her against his side. He pulled her left leg up and over his. "Is this okay?"

She couldn't get a single word out. Shadow nodded the tiniest bit against his chest.

Brent turned her face up slightly so he could see her eyes. "You look as though you're already asleep." Amazingly, he smiled. "Things will work out eventually. I promise."

He closed his eyes, easing into the mattress with familiarity. She breathed deeply, loving his scent, loving the way his presence soothed her, though why she was suddenly so afraid, she wasn't sure. She loved his strength, his pride. She loved him.

It was the last thought she had before she literally passed out.

6

"I WAS DRUGGED!"

The shout was shrill and piercing, filled with outrage. Brent wasn't quite quick enough to get his feet beneath him this time. He landed on the floor beside the bed, his naked body twisted in the blankets.

"What! *What?*"

Shadow hunched over on the mattress, her face in her hands. "Someone," she reiterated slowly, "drugged me."

"What the hell are you talking about?"

"Last night I couldn't keep my eyes open, couldn't think straight. I didn't want to go to bed, but I couldn't figure out how to tell you. This morning I understand, but last night I couldn't."

With a sigh, Brent ran his hand through his rumpled hair, then down his whiskered face. She had been exhausted, limp as a noodle when he'd carried her to bed. He shook his head. "How would someone do that?"

She looked at him and her expression was nearly blank with fear. "I don't know. It must have been in something I drank." She fretted her bottom lip with her teeth, twisted her hands in the sheet. "Maybe the eggnog. I'm the only one who drank it." Then her expression transformed, became so enraged, so mean, he blinked in surprise. "Someone," she growled, thumping the mattress with a fist, "got in here and *drugged my eggnog.*"

Pulling himself up from the floor gave Brent a moment to hide his grin. Damn, but she could be a ferocious little thing. He smoothed the covers, then sat beside her. After taking her hand, he said, "The doors haven't been opened. If they had, the alarm would have sounded. You're just stressed out from not getting enough sleep."

"I got enough sleep!"

"Then you're stressed out because you haven't yet made love with me. Hell, I know I'm stressed over it." He did grin this time. "We should remedy that."

"I know what I'm talking about, Brent. I'm a hard sleeper, but I don't pass out like that."

Brent gazed at her steadily, but in truth, he was distracted by her warm body, clothed only in the transparent teddy and held so close to his naked one. He said softly, "You'd been nervous about being with me and you were tense." He kissed her temple and said, "It'd been a really long time for you, and I know you came." In a teasing, somewhat bragging voice, he added, "That wasn't a wimpy little orgasm you had, but a mind-blower."

He waited and finally she said, "It was incredible." She twisted to look up at him. "You were incredible. I'm so sorry I fell asleep."

He tangled his hand in her hair, fitting his palm to her skull when she dropped her cheek to his chest. She smelled good, Brent thought, rubbing his nose against her neck, kissing a path to her ear. "You had a meltdown," he suggested. "It's nothing to be embarrassed about, sweetheart. I understand. Hell, I'm even a little proud."

She laughed, just as he'd intended. "You feel like strutting, do you?"

"You wanna know what I feel like doing?" He was still aroused from last night, and even her scream hadn't taken care of it. He was here with her, she was awake now and he wanted her. He was beginning to think he'd always want her.

Unfortunately, just as he started to kiss her, she seemed to become self-conscious. Brent allowed her to draw slightly away, but kept his arms around her shoulders.

"Brent, I still feel a little vague, and I...I need to, ah..."

It was odd, but Shadow managed to keep him on the verge of laughter, whether deliberately or not. His patience astounded him, but he had all morning and he planned to make use of it. He could afford to be patient just a little longer.

He gave her a smacking kiss. "Why don't you take a shower and see if that'll clear away the cobwebs? If you want, I could start some breakfast."

She was frowning, still apparently convinced she'd been drugged. But she said only, "Toast and coffee would be wonderful."

"Shadow?"

"Hmm?"

"Don't take too long."

"I won't."

A few minutes later, Brent heard the shower start. He found his pants and stepped into them, but didn't bother with his shirt or shoes. If he had his way, he would only be taking them off again soon.

Twice now. *Twice* he had slept with Shadow and not

made love to her. It had to be some kind of unbelievable record. But he wouldn't have missed either experience for the world. She was so much more than he'd first imagined. Too headstrong for her own good, with a kind of twisted, zany wisdom few people ever acquired.

She was sweet and serious, intelligent and nutty, by far the most sensuous woman he had ever known... who dressed in the most outlandish outfits. She would never be boring, but she would keep him on his toes.

No way in hell would he ever let anyone hurt her.

He obligingly started the coffee and placed a few slices of bread in the toaster. He set the table with butter, jam, cream and sugar. Then, remembering something he'd been meaning to do, he called his office.

His secretary seemed surprised by his order. "Yes, that's what I said. Two men. I don't care where you find them, but they can't work for me. Find someone from the other offices in the building. It's for the Love and Laughter contest, or some such. Just tell them to go to the little stretch of businesses I'm leasing over by the complexes. There's a shop there called Sex Appeal. They can pick up an application there."

Brent laughed, then added, "I was actually entered, but being as I own the property, if I won, I'd have to be disqualified." He hesitated, then smiled. "Why, thank you. The owner obviously thought I was a worthy contender, too, but she doesn't realize she's leasing from me. Now, don't forget we'll need two men." He chuckled again as he said, "She has to fill her quota."

Brent paced a few steps, one hand in his pocket. "Right. Thanks, Micky. I think that will do it. Why don't you clock out early today? Cancel any appointments I had this morning and reschedule them for Monday. Thanks."

He was still smiling slightly over Micky's comments when he turned and found Shadow standing there, utterly still, looking more vulnerable than he'd ever thought possible. *How much had she heard?*

She wore a long, man-size football jersey and nothing else. Her hair was damp, a mass of dark ringlets. She looked fresh and dewy and warm. Brent felt his body clench. "Feeling better?" he asked.

"I'm fine."

There was something oddly distant in her words and the way she said them. "There's coffee in the kitchen and I can have the toast ready in just a few minutes."

"Don't bother." She stared right at him and said, "I want you to leave now."

His jaw locked. *Damn.* "I don't think so, Shadow."

"Why not? Because you didn't get what you came for? I trusted you. I thought you cared a little about me." With each word, she became more rigid. "Why did you lie to me?"

"I never—"

She turned her back on him and walked away. Brent saw red. "I can't believe," he said very quietly, "that you're going to take this attitude today. Not after everything that happened last night."

"Last night wouldn't have happened at all if I'd known you were lying to me! You own my damn building!"

"So?" He propped his hands on his hips and his brows lowered in a fierce scowl. "You had to lease it from someone."

Her nose went into the air. "If it's not a big deal, then why didn't you tell me?"

"Stop shouting and maybe I'll explain."

She gave him a mutinous look. "I have to get dressed."

The morning had quickly deteriorated, and so had his temper. "Why? It looked to me as if you were willing to pick up where we left off. I imagine you don't even have anything on under that jersey, do you?"

She flushed. "Go to hell."

"You have to know how crazy that would make me. So why change your mind now?"

"Because now I'm mad. Now I know you lied to me." Her eyes were dark, dilated. "Until I know why, I'll feel much better fully dressed."

The quiet, deliberate closing of her bedroom door enraged him. Damn her, how could she turn so cold so quickly? Especially when he wanted her so much. Maybe, he thought, remembering her reserve of the night before, she was just stringing him along.

Granted, she couldn't have faked her exhaustion; she'd been dead to the world, her body lax, her deep breathing occasionally turning to soft snores. He almost smiled. No, she'd been totally wiped out, of that he was certain.

But she played a constant game of advance and retreat, and it was possible he'd fallen into a trap. A unique trap, but still a trap. It wasn't a very uplifting thought.

Brent waited until Shadow came out of the bedroom, then went in to dress. He emerged five minutes later, more collected, determined on his course. He would not be manipulated.

"I'm going to the office. If you settle down and want to talk calmly, give me a call." He didn't pay the least bit of attention to her sullen frown. "Also, the security people will be here today to finish installing the system." He looked at her directly, his expression hard. "Don't give them any trouble."

"Oh, don't worry. If I decide I don't want them here, I'll tell them so very nicely. I do tend to be nice, Brent. Remember?"

In two long strides he stood before her, her chin caught in his hand. "Too nice. Don't even think of flirting with some other guy to make me jealous, Shadow. I already told you I don't like games and you've played one too many already."

This time her tone was uncharacteristically solemn, and almost accusing. "I don't play games."

"No? What would you call this little tug-of-war with 'let's make love' and 'let's don't make love'? Normal procedure?"

Shadow looked down, then turned her back completely on him. "I'd call it the worst of luck. Or maybe the best." She was quiet a moment, then added in a sad whisper, "Please go, now."

"Shadow..." Brent didn't know what to say. Why the hell had he let his temper get the best of him? Not that it mattered now. He couldn't continue to let her lead him in circles. Still watching her averted profile, he shrugged on his coat. "I'll give you a call tonight to make certain everything went okay with the security people."

She didn't move, and Brent was forced to take her shoulders and turn her. She could have been carved in stone, her face was so still, her eyes so dull. He didn't like it. In fact, he hated it. "Be careful, and let me know if anything happens."

"The same refrain, Brent. I'm a big girl and I'm not stupid."

"No, but apparently you're someone's obsession. That means you have to be on guard." He left before he said anything else to upset her, but in his mind he knew the truth. *He* was obsessed, and the sensation got worse every day.

IT HAD BEEN A WISE decision to come to work. Not only had she managed to sort through all the new orders, she had perked up immensely.

Melancholy was for the birds. So Brent had lied? So what? He was like other men, after all, and that certainly shouldn't come as a shock.

But it did. Shadow couldn't help but chastise herself for handling the situation badly. She hadn't given him a chance to explain—if there was indeed an explanation.

She'd gotten hurt, and in the process, she'd ruined a very special morning. A morning that had held the potential for being the most memorable morning she'd ever been given.

Why was her timing so lousy with Brent? She was considering the vagaries of romance—hers in particular—when the phone rang. Kallie was busy with customers so Shadow picked it up herself.

"I've missed you."

Oh, no. That most definitely was not Brent's voice on the line. Very carefully, Shadow said, "I thought I'd seen the last of you."

There was a friendly, almost cheerful chuckle. "You aren't very observant. I saw you just today."

She gripped the receiver tightly. "Where?"

"On your way to work."

She bit her lip, trying to remember any cars she'd passed, any people she'd seen on the way.

"You're wearing a shirt that has vultures on the front. And I like the tight jeans. You look really cute."

The day had been a disaster and she was still berating herself over her part in it. She had no tolerance or patience for this right now. "Look, I've about had it with you. I think you're childish and awfully annoying. Do us both a favor and leave me alone." She slammed the phone down so hard the items on her desk rattled.

So he hadn't given up, after all. She considered Brent's earlier instructions, to call if anything happened. Damned if she would.

She was capable. She *wanted* Brent, but she didn't *need* him.

The snow started coming down around three o'clock and by six everything was blanketed in white. They announced a traveler's advisory, so Shadow decided to close the shop early.

To be on the safe side, she notified the security guard and he happily gave her escort to her car. He even waited until she was well on her way before moving on. The salt trucks hadn't had a chance to cover all the roads yet so Shadow drove slowly and very cautiously. For the first time in a long time, she dreaded going home to an empty house. She blamed Brent for that, for showing her how nice it was having him around.

And the stupid phone call had unsettled her more than she liked. She realized whoever it was must have gotten close enough to the shop to see her, because anytime she'd been outside and visible, she'd been wearing her coat. How could he possibly have known about the vultures on her sweatshirt? It made her uneasy.

The temperature dropped rapidly. Forecasters predicted a low of ten degrees, and that wasn't taking into account the windchill factor. Shadow turned the heater up a notch and squeezed her arms close to her body. It was bitterly cold, no two ways about it.

Distracted, she watched the houses to her left as she passed Brent's place, trying to determine, out of sheer curiosity and nosiness, if he was home. She almost ran the red light, but the roads were pretty much deserted, so it really wouldn't have mattered. Still, habit had her hitting the brakes and going into a full slide.

Right off the road and into the ditch.

The car rocked to a halt against a snowbank and Shadow slammed her hand onto the steering wheel in a fit of anger. "My luck can't be this bad!"

She made an effort to rock the car out, but it was good and stuck, and probably would be until she hired a tow truck to drag her out.

Going over her options took all of about three seconds. Her house was still a good walking distance away, while Brent's was right there, once you trod the long drive to the front door. Pride had its place, but compared with freezing, it was less than nothing.

Snowflakes as big as cotton balls covered her head the minute she stepped from the car. The snow was already so deep her ankles disappeared in the frozen drifts. Tucking her hands into her pockets, Shadow lowered her face to protect it from the force of the gusting wind and headed for Brent's driveway.

The chattering of her teeth should have announced her arrival. When it obviously didn't, Shadow lifted one snow-covered foot and kicked the door soundly. No way was she going to remove her hands from the dubious warmth of her pockets simply to give a polite knock.

But she was worried. The house was dark, not a single light on that she could tell. Whatever would she do if Brent wasn't home? If she could be certain he didn't have an alarm system himself, she would gladly break in. But then it wasn't necessary. Brent opened the door a moment later, a dim flashlight in his hand. He looked as if he'd been deep in thought, his face a shadowy mask of fatigue. Or was that worry?

Grabbing her arm, Brent pulled her in the door, then slammed it shut. He began brushing snow from her head, her shoulders. "Where the hell have you been?"

Shadow blinked, trying to stop her shivers, but unable to. Brent cursed, then dragged her into his arms, squeezing her tight for just a moment before taking her hand and hurrying her through his house and into the family room.

It was immense, filled with posh leather furnishings and highly polished, heavy wood tables. An elaborate marble fireplace dominated an entire wall and in it was a huge, raging fire, the heat emanating in waves.

Brent dragged a wing chair near the blaze and gently pushed Shadow into it. Dropping to his knees before her, he began removing her wet shoes and socks.

"Are you nuts, Shadow? What the hell are you doing out in this storm? I thought you were staying home. I've been calling your house since the storm started."

Through chattering teeth, she said, "I was upset. I needed something to do other than sitting around the house moping. So I went in to work."

Brent held her frozen toes in his palms, trying to warm her. "You were upset?"

Nodding, Shadow answered truthfully. "I don't like being mad at you, Brent."

Brent looked at her for a long moment, then stood.

"Take off those jeans. They're wet clear up to your knees. I'm going to get you a drink and a blanket."

Shadow did as he bade her, mostly because the wet pants were uncomfortably cold. She had her bare feet stretched out toward the fire, wiggling her toes to warm them, when Brent returned. He handed her a glass of whiskey, which she promptly set aside, then she watched, fascinated as he spread a large quilt before the fire and laid another at the bottom of it.

"Come on, sit here where you can feel the fire."

"Brent, why is it so dark in here?"

"The electricity is out on the whole street. A result of the storm. And unfortunately, the heating was all re-done with the remodeling. I now have electric heat, which means the house is going to cool off consider-ably as the night goes on."

Shadow had no sooner stood than Brent began pull-ing off her coat. "This is wet, too. You'll feel better without it."

She blushed when Brent's gaze went to her shirt and stayed there a long moment. Finally, he smiled.

"I was thinking of you," she explained, "when I changed to go to work this morning."

Two vultures adorned the front of her shirt. Sitting on a barren branch, their expressions sullen, one said, "Patience, hell. I'm gonna kill somebody." Brent chuckled even as he lowered Shadow to the quilt, then tucked the extra blanket around her. "I hope it wasn't my death you were anticipating."

His soft, husky words sent a tingle down her spine. "No. My impatience for something else entirely." She smiled up into his green eyes, the reflection of the fire sending mysterious shadows to dance in them. "Brent, why didn't you tell me you owned my building?"

He leaned forward to place a gentle kiss on her forehead. "I knew that would disqualify me from your little contest and at first I wanted to use the contest as an excuse to get to know you better. And then I suppose I was...concerned that you might treat me differently if you knew you were leasing from me. Personal finances have a way of influencing how people treat each other."

Incredulous, Shadow demanded, "You thought I might cozy up to you just because you hold my lease?"

He gently tucked an errant curl behind her ear. Her hair was damp from her walk in the snow, her cheeks and nose still very cold. "I know now that you wouldn't."

"But you think I would deliberately lead you on, then pull back before making love to you?"

He sighed. "I was mad, Shadow. I didn't mean half of what I said, and I almost immediately regretted saying it." He flopped onto his back beside her and closed his eyes. He wore a T-shirt, even as cool as the house was, and Shadow could see the definition of his chest, his strength and power. The shirt stretched taut over his broad shoulders. "You're tearing me apart, honey. I've never felt so damn on edge before."

With her heartbeat racing and her body quickly warming, Shadow moved so she loomed over him. "I think I'm in love with you, Brent."

That got his eyes open in a hurry. Before he could speak, Shadow laid her fingers against his mouth. "Just listen. If I sometimes seem contrary, or like I'm giving off mixed signals, you should realize I'm a little confused, too. It's been an awfully long time since anyone made me feel the way you do. In fact, I don't think I've ever felt this way. And I've only just decided I might like it. So," she said, laying her heart on the line, "would you like to make love with me, Brent? Now?"

Brent's answer was a low groan and a sudden movement of his body that had Shadow flat on her back, the blankets shoved aside and the warmth of his hands and mouth touching her everywhere. He'd never been like this before, wild and frenzied. Usually he was so methodical and thorough in his lovemaking, but now he was ravenous. Shadow grinned at that thought, but it fit. Brent seemed intent on devouring her, quickly, before she could change her mind.

As if she would?

Certainly not, not when it was so wonderful. The cool air didn't faze her when her shirt was thrown aside, and she was instantly imbued with heat at the touch of his tongue on her nipple, the nip of his teeth.

He reared back and jerked his shirt over his head, tossing it away. With shaking, fumbling fingers, he worked the snap and zipper on his jeans. Shadow reached out, cupping her hand beneath his testicles, holding him gently, and his breath hissed out while his eyes squeezed shut.

"I've waited too long," he muttered through his teeth, then pushed her hand away and shoved his pants down. Shadow wanted to touch him, to measure him with her fingers and stroke him and explore him, but he didn't give her a chance.

He stripped her panties from her body, then positioned himself between her thighs. For a long moment he knelt there, frozen, looking at her, his hands on her thighs holding her open. His chest labored; his nostrils flared. "No matter what," he said, "this time we finish things. I don't give a damn if the house burns down."

"Yes." Shadow reached for him, but he caught her

hands and held them near her chest. With his free hand, he stroked her, just riffling his fingers through her curls, teasing her.

He glanced at her face. "You like that?"

"Brent..." She liked it so much, she couldn't take it. "Make love to me."

"I am." His fingers went deep, easing inside her body, stretching her. He used his thumb to stroke her clitoris until her hips were lifting and she could do no more than gasp.

He released her hands so he could feel her breasts, and Shadow used the moment to clutch at him, to try to drag him down to her. "Here," he said, rubbing her left nipple between finger and thumb, "and here." His other thumb teased between her thighs. "These are the two most sensitive places on your body."

The rough pad of his thumb tormented her, rasping her delicate, swollen flesh while two of his long fingers stayed pressed deep inside her. He leaned down, slowly, adding to her tension, heightening her anticipation, and licked her nipple. "I love how soft and warm you feel in my mouth." His gaze heated, locked on to hers. "Here," he whispered, "and *here*."

Her body arched, the orgasm taking her by surprise. Brent stayed close, watching her, breathing hard while whispering encouragement.

The pleasure finally ebbed and Brent came up and over her, holding himself away on stiffened arms. She saw that he was desperately trying to get himself under control.

She didn't want control. She wanted him wild and eager, as eager as she herself had been. She said, only half teasing, "Don't make me get rough with you,

Brent. Enough is enough. I want you now. This minute."

The sound he made was part laugh, part groan, but there was no indecision in his actions. He snagged his slacks, retrieved his wallet and located a condom. He held it up for her to see. "I've been hopeful," he said, giving her a heated look as he rolled it on, letting Shadow watch in fascination.

Holding her knees apart, he lowered himself between her thighs, his gaze never leaving hers. Then slowly, with one long thrust, he pushed into her body.

Shadow was enthralled. Even though it was difficult accommodating his size, nothing had ever felt so right. Without even thinking, she wrapped her legs around his hips and held him tight. Brent tipped his head back, squeezed his eyes shut. The cords of his neck were drawn taut, his shoulders rigid. His chest heaved, but he held perfectly still and Shadow instinctively knew he was fighting to keep it from ending too soon.

"I've just made up my mind," she whispered. "I love you, Brent. I really do."

His arms collapsed, his face coming down beside hers, a loud groan sounding in her ear. And then he was thrusting heavily into her. The friction was exquisite, the unbelievable feelings rapidly building again. Shadow wrapped her arms around him and held on.

He pounded into her and a moment later she climaxed. Even through her own pleasure, Shadow heard the sounds of Brent exploding with her, his moans low and guttural and real. It pleased her and she told him again, louder this time, that she loved him.

It was sometime later when the uncomfortable coolness of the room forced them to move. Shadow was beginning to shiver now that her body was no longer heated, was instead languid and relaxed and nearly asleep. Brent raised himself to his elbows to look down at her. There was an unfathomable intensity in his gaze, but he kissed her gently on her parted lips, then rolled to the side.

Shadow immediately followed, curling against him for his warmth. He obligingly put his arm beneath her, tugging her close, then kicked and shuffled until he reached the blanket and could pull it over them both.

Shadow asked, "Are we going to sleep here?"

Brent didn't answer her at first, then he asked, "Do you want to? It's too cold for you to try to go home. And this will be the warmest room in the house."

After yawning, Shadow explained, "I couldn't go home now, anyway. My car is in the ditch. That's why I ended up here in the first place."

Brent went curiously still, then repeated, "Your car is in a ditch?"

Nodding, Shadow said, "I was on my way home from work, tried to stop at a red light and slid right off the road."

"How far away?"

She didn't understand the suspicion in his tone, but was too tired to worry about it anyway. "Nearly in front of your house, actually."

Brent twisted around to face her. "Tomorrow, we're really going to find your car in a ditch?"

Shadow frowned at him. "Unless someone steals it tonight. But in this storm, I think that's unlikely."

Brent scowled in thought, but his hand idly, almost automatically stroked Shadow's hip. Staring down at the top of her breasts, he said, "You know, Shadow, you didn't need an excuse to come by. I want us to be at ease with each other. If you wanted to apologize, you could have just called and not gone out in this weather."

Eyes narrowing slightly, Shadow asked, "Apologize? I didn't apologize, Brent. And I wasn't looking for an excuse to come by." Enunciating carefully, as if he were dim-witted, Shadow explained, "I was on my way home from work. Granted, I was looking over at your house as I passed, which is probably why I didn't see the red light right off, but I didn't land my car—a car I love—in a ditch, just to have a reason to come by. In fact," she added as he started to speak, "I wouldn't have come here if I could have made it home in this storm."

"Shadow..." He faltered at her antagonistic look, but then blundered on. "Honey, I'm glad you're here. Really. But I'd rather you just admit—"

Shadow sat up to glare at him. The blanket fell over her lap and covered most of her legs, bent beneath her. He didn't say another word, his eyes glued to her exposed breasts and belly. He reached out to touch her, his eyes going all smoky again. Shadow didn't move, but she did say, "Please, Brent. Finish enlightening me on what I ought to admit."

He caught her arms and pulled her down to his chest. "Admit you love me. Again."

Startled, Shadow said, "That wasn't what you were going to say."

"No, but neither am I going to get into another argument with you. Unbelievable coincidences happen all the time, and besides that, at the moment, I don't care how it is you came to be here. I'm just glad you did."

Well, put like that, how could she stay mad? She'd convince him in the morning that she hadn't fabricated a reason to see him. Right now, he had his large hands spread over her backside, holding her close to his rapidly hardening body. Arguing with Brent was invigorating, but making love with him most definitely had it beat.

HE'D NEVER IMAGINED sleeping on a floor could be so relaxing. For the first time in weeks, he felt replete, all his tension—mostly sexual—melted away. He'd awakened several times during the night, but not because of the hard floor. Shadow's softness, her enticing scent, had interrupted his sleep. She was finally with him, beside him, in his house. He took incredible satisfaction in having her here and he couldn't keep himself from reaching for her again and again. He'd never enjoyed a sleepless night more. He'd never enjoyed a woman more.

Even now her hair tickled his chin and one small hand lay open over his heart. More than that, her silky thigh rested on his lap, making his erection twitch with her every breath. That same incredible need of the night before rushed through him, but he didn't move, content to simply lie back and enjoy her, having her near, feeling her warm breath brushing his skin.

When Shadow finally awoke, she did so loudly, a rough, heartfelt groan emerging as she stretched her body against his. With each muscle she moved, she moaned anew, and Brent suffered a twinge of pity for her. He had been rather relentless last night; but then, so had she.

Suddenly she went very still. Cautiously, slowly, she raised herself on one elbow. Brent pretended to be asleep. He could feel her peering down at him, knew her eyes were wide, her breath held. He was hard-pressed not to smile. When her hand touched him, gently inquisitive, he barely resisted the urge to cover her again. She explored him with a tentative curiosity that had his muscles tightening in anticipation.

Sitting up more fully, Shadow inadvertently pulled the covers from Brent's lower body. At least he thought it had been an accident. But when she made no move to rectify the situation, Brent had to assume her gaze was somewhere south of his abdomen. He could picture her, the intensity of her expression, and suddenly it wasn't enough. He peeked at her, and sure enough, she was studying his hard-on. Closely.

Leaning forward, her beautiful, heavy breasts very near his ribs, she scrutinized him. His hands were already above his head, a typical sleeping position for Brent. But now he locked his fingers together, fighting the urge to return her interest.

He heard a small chuckle and Shadow said, "Quit playing possum, Brent. I know you're awake."

Looking at her lazily, he smiled. "I didn't want to inhibit your...explorations."

He felt her fingers curl warmly around him, bolder now, but he kept his eyes on her face, watching her watch the movement of her hand. It was innocently erotic. It made him insane.

"You don't mind that I'm curious?"

"Not at all." His words sounded like a croak. Out of self-preservation, Brent closed his eyes again, but that only heightened his awareness of her fingers stroking him, her warm breath on his belly. He jumped when she began talking again.

"I liked what you did last night. Where you kissed me."

His entire being clenched with the memory of her sweet taste, her spicy scent. "I liked it, too."

"Would you...like it if I kissed you?"

His heart threatened to come through his chest. "Yes."

"I never have before, but then...I never knew you."

Undone by her words, her sincerity, he tensed. He felt her settle beside him, one hand still holding him, the other stretched over his belly. He had to touch her, even though he feared breaking the moment, and he reached down to tangle his right hand in her hair. "Shadow. If you feel uncomfortable, I wouldn't want...*oh, God.*"

He couldn't think straight—all his concentration centered on maintaining control and enjoying the soft, moist warmth of her mouth for as long as he could. She tasted him, not tentatively—licking, then gently taking the head of his penis in her mouth and sucking.

His hips arched from the floor and he cursed, struggling for some faint measure of control. Rather than pull away when she felt his response, she drew him deeper, her tongue curling around him as her hand curled, tighter, holding him still, consuming him. A ragged groan broke past his clenched teeth and she made a responding sound of pleasure.

It was too much. He tugged her away, not giving her time to complain about his sudden actions. He drew her up and under him.

His fingers slid over her, once, twice. He hadn't taken the proper time to prepare her, but she was ready for him, wet and swollen, hot. He knew she'd enjoyed what she'd done to him and that only added to his urgency. He thrust into her, hard, deep, and knew it was all over for him.

It was unbelievable, undeniable and a bit frightening. Brent couldn't stop kissing her. Even as he thrust that final time, his whole body straining with his release, he felt he couldn't get enough of her, his hands wanting to be filled with her breasts, his nostrils hungry for the scent of her, needing her taste in his mouth. It was the gentle movements of Shadow's hands on his shoulders that finally brought him some measure of reason.

Releasing his hold on her slightly, he gained enough coherence to ask, "Are you okay?"

He could feel her smile. "After all that? After having my body explode into a million pieces? I think my head may have shot off somewhere. Is it still on my shoulders?"

He leaned up to smile at her. They were both sweaty, and Shadow's hair was a damp tangle. Her eyes were puffy from sleep, her lips puffy from his kisses. She was by far the most beautiful woman he'd ever seen. "Are you telling me," he asked, touching her ear, her jaw, "that you enjoyed yourself?"

"*Enjoyed* is an inadequate word." Her eyes drifted over him lazily. "You're wonderful, Brent. It's rather obvious why I love you."

The first time she'd said it, she'd startled him. He hadn't remarked on it, taking it as one of those female things that got said at various moments. Now he wondered if it could be true. Either way, he liked the sound of it. He managed enough strength to raise one brow a good inch. "Oh? And why is it you love me?"

"Your body, of course. And your stamina. Do all men make love so voraciously?"

He closed his eyes on a wave of emotion. "You really must have had lousy taste in men." He sighed, looked at her and said, "I would think any man who touched you would be the same. They were obviously idiots."

She gave him a fat smile. "This is kind of neat, isn't it?"

"What?"

"Lying here, still a part of each other, making small talk. There's only one problem."

"You mean other than the fact we don't have any heat or electricity, and I'm starving and desperately in need of a hot shower, and we're most probably snowed in?"

"Yes. Other than all that."

Brent felt his eyes widen suddenly. "Oh, hell. I just realized the problem."

Shadow waited, her look one of keen interest.

"We didn't use anything."

"Use anything?"

"Protection. I don't suppose you're on the pill?"

She snorted at him. "Whatever for? I told you it had been seven years."

"I know, but..." But what? he wondered. Shadow wasn't the average modern woman. She wasn't average in any way. "Damn, sweetheart, I'm sorry. I've never, absolutely *never* done anything so irresponsible. You took me by surprise, showing up here yesterday. I just lost control." He groaned. "I don't believe I just said that. I never lose control."

She looked skeptical at that, but kept quiet.

"And then you gave me that sweet story about accidentally going into a ditch...."

Her hands on his shoulders tightened, her fingers biting into his flesh. "What," she asked with quiet menace, "is so sweet about me landing in a ditch?"

Brent didn't want to get into any of that; she was

here and he was glad, however it had happened. He said again, "I'm sorry."

She raised one hand to touch his cheek. "It doesn't matter. I told you, I love you. Besides, that's not the problem I was talking about." She hesitated, then asked, "Do you love me?"

Brent stared at her, his guts cramping. "Shadow..." He didn't know what to say. Love? Hell, he didn't know. The practical side of him told him it was impossible. They hadn't known each other long enough to be in love.

Shadow moved restlessly. "Never mind."

"Honey, don't." He felt panicked by the look in her dark eyes, and he hated it. "Don't shy away from me."

"I didn't mean to put you on the spot. I guess I was being too forward again."

"No." He said it urgently, wanting her to understand. "You're being you. And I care a great deal about you, Shadow. But...love? I..."

The shrill ringing of the phone kept Brent from stammering around further and making a complete ass of himself. He rolled to Shadow's side, then reached for the phone on the small table set next to the chair.

"Hello?"

"She's there, isn't she!" The voice was male, anxious and angry. "She spent the night with you, didn't she?"

"Who is this?" Brent demanded, drawing into a sitting position, his muscles rigid.

Low and mean, almost sulky, the voice dropped in pitch. "She doesn't need you! Besides, I found her first and she's mine. You remember that!" And the line went dead.

7

"WHAT IS IT?"

Brent feigned a casual shrug, avoiding her eyes. "Nothing."

"Oh? Then why were you cursing a blue streak and why are you frowning and grinding your teeth?" As Shadow asked that, she stood, wrapping one blanket around herself. It was getting colder by the moment, and she needed to make a trip to Brent's bathroom. The thought of putting on her clothes, still rumpled on the floor from the night before and no doubt cold to boot, had her shivering in earnest.

Brent had kept the fire going all night, getting up between lovemaking to add more wood. It took Shadow a minute to untangle her bra from her shirt; Brent had pulled them both off together, without unfastening anything. Then she hooked it across the brass handles on the fireplace screen to warm it.

Brent stared. "I wasn't grinding my teeth or... Shadow, what the hell are you doing?"

She now had each item of her clothing hanging from some part of the fireplace. "I'm warming them," she explained. "Have you ever put your chest into a cold bra? It isn't very pleasant."

"I can imagine." He tried to figure some way to get her out of the room for just a moment. He wanted to call the police. Actually, he wanted to get hold of the bastard hounding her and beat some sense into him. Since that option wasn't open to him, he would have to try the police. This was getting to be too damned much. Surely the police could do something.

Shadow saved him from finding a believable excuse for privacy when she asked where his bathroom could be found. Brent remembered with some satisfaction that they'd never made it beyond the family room. She hadn't seen the rest of his house.

The tour he gave her was necessarily short and quick. Shadow was shaking and her knees were locked together. Brent showed her into his bathroom, massive compared to her own, complete with an overhead skylight and Jacuzzi tub. He'd located a pair of his sweats for her to put on in lieu of her cold, wrinkled clothing, and showed her where to find a toothbrush and towels. There was probably enough hot water left in the water heater to supply a basic washing, so Brent assumed he'd have a few minutes to himself to make his call.

The cold was more of an inducement for speed than he had reckoned. He was in midconversation, with no way to terminate the call other than hanging up on the officer, when Shadow came back into the room, sat herself in front of the fire and began brushing the tangles from her hair.

There was nothing for it but to let her hear. He hadn't wanted to worry her. He wanted to protect her. Then he realized that, even though she listened, she didn't look particularly worried.

She even interjected at one point, "I got a call yesterday, also. He called the shop and described to me what I was wearing. He must have gotten close and looked in the window, since I had my coat buttoned anytime I went outside."

The officer was forgotten, the phone hanging from Brent's hand. "You what? Why the hell didn't you tell me that sooner?"

She glanced up at him and shrugged. "The same reason you didn't tell me who called a few minutes ago, I suppose. I didn't want to worry you." She went back to brushing her hair. "By the way, my caller ID said 'unknown.'"

Brent was furious. He finished his conversation with the officer, accepting the assurance that someone would get back to them soon. But he knew there was nothing that could be done.

He stalked around the family room attempting to get a handle on his temper. He'd pulled on sweats, too, but he knew his hair was in bad need of a comb and there was dark stubble shadowing his face. Shadow watched him. He imagined he looked pretty scruffy at the moment, which could explain the intensity of her interest.

Finally, he went to stand before her, staring down at her in reproach. "I can't believe you didn't say anything about that bastard calling you. Did he threaten you?"

She laid the brush aside. "Nope. He repeated what I was wearing and said I was cute. I hung up on him."

Brent went down on his knees before her, his hands on her thighs. He said with as much stern sobriety as he could muster, "You had no business driving in to work alone yesterday."

"He called me at work, not before."

Brent ignored her interruption. "And beyond that, you had no business putting your car in a ditch and allowing yourself to be alone—at night—where he could have grabbed you."

"Brent." Her sigh was long and impatient. "We

don't know that he plans to 'grab' me. So far he's only been an aggravation. And I don't know what choice I had about coming here once my car was stuck. I couldn't very well sit in the damn thing and freeze, waiting to see if anyone came by. And going to my house would have taken much longer."

She leaned past Brent to pull on her shoes. Brent realized he was grinding his teeth again, stopped abruptly, then gave her a look of strained patience.

"You should never have put yourself in that situation in the first place."

"I did not," she said, "ditch my car on purpose just to have an excuse to see you. That would be lame and pathetic and dishonest."

Running an agitated hand through his hair, Brent replied reasonably, "You said your car is right in front of my house? Isn't that one hell of a coincidence, Shadow?"

She watched him a moment longer, then stood. "You're making me very angry again, Brent."

"I just want complete honesty between us. That's all.... Now what do you think you're doing?"

"Going home." She shrugged into her coat. "You're totally unreasonable and I don't enjoy being accused of something I didn't do."

"Aw, damn it...wait a minute!" He stepped in front of her when she headed for the door. "You can't walk home in this weather."

"It's stopped snowing."

"But it must be a foot deep out there."

"That's an exaggeration. I'd say not more than half a foot." She poked him in the chest. "So get out of my way."

"No."

"No?"

Brent had never witnessed such an incredulous and outraged expression. He wanted to pull her into his arms and kiss the frown from her forehead. He said instead, "Be reasonable, sweetheart. There's no way I'm going to let you walk home alone in this weather. And don't forget about your secret admirer. He may be watching for you. It's stupid to even think of going out there."

"So now I'm stupid?"

He barely caught her arm as she started past again. Unable to help himself, he chuckled. "For such a small woman, you take incredibly long, stomping strides when you're angry." She tried to resist him, but he finally got her into the circle of his arms. "Give me a break, sweetheart. I'm only a man. And last night was enough to leave anyone fuddled. This morning I even forgot to wear a rubber. I've never forgotten myself like that before. Do you realize I could have gotten you pregnant?"

Shadow raised her chin. "I don't care. I told you, I want children before I get too old."

"Thirty-one is not old, Shadow. There's plenty of time yet to do things the right way."

"I disagree," she said mutinously, "because every time I'm around you, you manage to enrage me."

"But you love me?"

"Rather proves I'm not as intelligent as I claimed, doesn't it? Now, let me go. I'm leaving."

Brent readied himself for battle. His mouth was already open, loaded with convincing arguments, when the doorbell rang. His teeth clicked shut with a snap and he gripped her shoulders. "Stay right here. Don't move."

Shadow proceeded to ignore him, following him to the front door. "You might own a lot of businesses, and I guess you're used to being in charge. But you're not my boss, Brent. Nor will you ever be my boss. I wish you'd try to accept that."

Highly harassed, Brent opened the door.

It took him a moment to believe his eyes, and then he wanted to groan, or quite literally find a hole to sink into. He wasn't given a chance to do either. "Brent, sweetheart! Thank goodness you're home!" Joan flew through the door in a flurry of white fur. Her hat, coat, even her gloves were trimmed in white ermine. She was tall, slender, and at the moment wrapped firmly around him.

Doing his best to disengage himself and close the door at the same time, Brent looked to Shadow. "Ah, Shadow, this is Joan Howard."

"I'm not leaving," Shadow stated.

It was such an about-face, Brent grinned, and finally managed, thanks to the length of his arms, to set Joan a good distance away from his person.

Joan began explaining, a pitiful expression on her lovely face, "I had to spend the night in the most horrible little hotel. The roads were awful. They've only just now become passable. I would have called last night, but the storm disrupted the phone lines somehow, and it was impossible." She drew to a halt, a beautiful smile appearing. "Oh, Brent. It's so good to see you again."

Trying once more to lock herself in his arms, Joan seemed distressed by his quick maneuvering, which put him out of range. He said easily, reaching for Shadow, "I want you to meet my..."

His what? He turned to Shadow in a silent bid for assistance, but she only blinked slowly at him. Then, to his immense relief, she came to his side.

Sticking her hand out and smiling enigmatically, Shadow explained, "I'm Shadow Callahan. I spent the night."

Joan straightened, her nose a good two inches in the air as she stared down at Shadow's rumpled form. "Whatever for?"

"Whatever...?" Shadow laughed, turning to Brent to ask incredulously, "Is this the woman you were engaged to?"

"Uh...yeah."

"And she doesn't understand why I spent the night? Why, shame on you, Brent." Shadow smacked him playfully. "You weren't really putting your all into that engagement, now were you?"

Brent nearly choked. "I...we—"

Shadow waved him to silence. "Never mind." Turning back to Joan, she asked, "Won't you come in? It's dreadfully cold outside. Of course, it's not much warmer in here."

Joan walked, dumbfounded, at Shadow's side, her arm held securely. Shadow continued to chatter, obviously enjoying Brent's moment of distress. "Brent's electricity went out. We had to sleep on the floor in front of the fireplace. And even then it was chilly. Of course, Brent is always so warm...but you'd know that, wouldn't you?"

Joan stopped abruptly, digging in her expensive leather boot heels. She jerked away from Shadow, confronted Brent with her hands on her hips and demanded, "Whoever is this woman and why would you have her here?"

Brent took a lesson from Shadow's book and answered, "She's here because I want her here. I can't seem to keep my hands off her."

Joan actually reeled. "That's disgustingly crude!"

"Actually," Shadow confided, "it wasn't. It was wonderful."

Nostrils flaring delicately, Joan ignored Shadow, and said, "You'd better explain yourself, Brent."

Brent rapidly became irritated. "You're welcome to stay and warm yourself, Joan, but you should understand up front that I won't hear any insults or slurs on Shadow. If you can't behave politely, you may as well leave."

Joan huffed. "When did you plan to tell me about her?"

"I didn't. My relationship with Shadow is none of your business. But you probably would have met her over Christmas. She's coming to Chicago for a visit then."

"You must be joking! Your parents would have a fit."

Shadow laughed. Loudly. It was actually quite rude, but Brent only smiled fondly at her. She said, "Martin and Debra were the ones who invited me."

"You're lying."

Brent was shocked into silence. Immediately he swiveled his gaze to Shadow, leery of how she might retaliate to such a blatant insult. To his surprise, she laughed all the more.

"Joan, you really are funny."

She huffed again. Staring down her nose at Shadow, she breathed in her haughtiest tone, "I beg your pardon?"

"Oh, that's okay. No harm done. Desperate words from a desperate woman. I didn't take offense."

Brent had to fight to hold in his laughter. Joan looked confused by Shadow, and Shadow appeared smug, if a little sympathetic. He asked her quietly, "To the victor goes the spoils?"

Shadow slanted him a look. "If the victor wants them. Which at this moment she's not at all certain she does."

"Of course you do. You love me, remember?"

Joan shook her head as if to clear it, then remarked, "This is absurd."

By silent agreement, they ventured into the family room, the only warm room in the house. Joan drew up short at the sight of Shadow's bra and other clothing stretched about the fireplace. Brent cleared his throat, but Shadow grinned. She really was enjoying herself, he realized.

"I don't suppose you could scrounge up something for breakfast, could you, Brent? I'm starving," she exclaimed.

Brent eyed Shadow's relaxed pose in the chair, then glanced at Joan, sitting rigidly on the very edge of her seat. She looked provoked and ready to do serious damage to somebody. He decided Shadow could better defend herself than he could, and agreed to figure out breakfast.

But he rushed it, not willing to press his luck.

SHADOW GAVE JOAN a moment to acclimate herself to the situation. It was rather sad, she thought, that a woman would feel compelled to chase a man. Shadow hoped she would have more pride should such a circumstance ever occur to her. Any failed relationships she'd had she'd been more than thrilled to see the end of. But Brent? Well, she didn't think she would ever be truly content away from him. She loved him.

Brent had said Joan only wanted him for his money, but Shadow needed to know if that was true. She watched dispassionately as Joan seemed to gather herself, her haughtiness returning with a vengeance. She stood, removed her ermine coat and hat, then tossed them on the chair. Pacing the room, she eyed Shadow's clothes on the fireplace with distaste.

"As you can see," Shadow said easily, "my clothes were wet and cold last night when I arrived. I put them there to warm them so I could dress. But then Brent gave me some sweats to put on. They're really comfortable, even though they're too big. I had to roll the waistband up three times to make the pants fit. But I like the top being so large."

Joan gave her a look of great dislike. "Do you have to rattle on like that? I'm trying to think."

"About what?"

Joan ignored her question to ask one of her own. "How long have you known Brent?"

"Not long really. A couple of weeks."

"Good. He should be tiring of you soon, then. He did this all the time in Chicago. Had his little flings. I tolerated it, of course, but once we marry, it will stop."

Shadow felt her chin drop. Incredulous, she asked, "You didn't mind if he was unfaithful to you?"

Joan lifted one elegant shoulder. "It's the way he does things. He must always be in control, which means forever proving to me where my place is. He's always made up to me later by buying me something exquisite." She dangled her bracelet for Shadow to see. "This is a little something he gave me before he left Chicago."

Brent entered at that moment, saying, "Actually, it was about three months before I left. An apology, I believe it was, for breaking off with you."

Joan visibly jerked at his entrance, and Shadow knew that everything Joan had told her was a lie. Joan was watching Brent warily, her gaze occasionally flicking toward Shadow, waiting, probably, to find out if her lies would be revealed. Shadow said, "It's a beautiful bracelet. And it looks lovely on you."

It had likely cost a small fortune, Shadow thought, looking at the diamond-encrusted gold bracelet. It was fashioned like a tennis bracelet, but heavier, the diamonds so large the bracelet would have very little flexibility. It should have adorned a queen, not an everyday, average woman. Shadow couldn't imagine ever putting something so lavish and expensive on her own arm. It wouldn't go with her jeans.

She noticed Brent watching her and smiled. "What did you round up for food? After all our...exertions, I'm ready to faint from hunger."

Brent was silent for just a moment, then carried the tray toward her. "The electricity is still out, so all I have is fruit and juice, some cold bagels and jam. Will that do for now?"

Rolling her eyes in bliss, Shadow said, "Sounds delicious," then added politely, "Joan, would you like something? Brent must still be in a state of uncertainty. Otherwise, I'm sure he would have remembered his manners and made the offer himself."

Joan turned to Brent, a disbelieving frown marring her smooth brow. "I can't believe you tolerate this, tolerate her! She's unbelievably crass and outspoken."

Shadow saw Brent's eyes narrow in anger, and she quickly waved him to silence, concerned about what he might do. Around a mouthful of bagel, she explained, "He likes it that I'm outspoken. And unbelievably enough, he doesn't think me crass—at least not often."

Brent walked over and shoved the bagel back into Shadow's mouth. "Eat. I'll speak for myself if you don't mind."

He faced Joan. "If you came here thinking there was some way we could reconcile, I'm sorry. But I made it clear in Chicago that it was over. As you see, I'm very much involved with Shadow, and that's not going to change with your presence."

"She's a distraction, an oddity," Joan said finally, her tone filled with spite. "You'll tire of her soon enough. In the meantime, I think I'll stick around." She picked up her coat and headed for the door, sending a look of pure dislike toward Shadow, who merely waved, taking another drink of her juice.

Joan said from the doorway, "I'll keep in touch," then stormed out.

Shadow chided Brent, "You should have escorted her to the door to see her out."

"She's a malicious bitch. She can see herself out."

Shadow chuckled. "Aw, poor baby. You really let her get to you, didn't you?"

Brent stiffened. "It's not funny, Shadow. It was bad enough in Chicago, but now she's following me here?"

Shadow set her glass of juice on the tray and went to Brent, crawling, uninvited, into his lap. Despite his stiff posture, she wiggled around until she was comfortable, then gave him a hug. "I'm sorry. I suppose I should be more sympathetic."

"Yes, you should." He relaxed enough to loop his

arms loosely around her. "She's a pain in the butt, and I won't tolerate her insulting you."

"Brent, I didn't pay any attention to that. It was just jealousy. If it weren't for you, someone like Joan wouldn't even have noticed me, much less made the effort to comment on my behavior or appearance. It's a beautiful day. Don't let her spoil it."

Brent rubbed his face in agitation. "A beautiful day? There's not a single color visible outside other than white, it's probably ten degrees, if that, we've had a maniac call to threaten you and another maniac show up to annoy me, and we have no electricity. This is a beautiful day?"

Shadow kissed his jaw. She slipped her hand beneath the rounded neckline of his sweatshirt. "You're not using the right perspective. You're seeing things all wrong."

His skin heated, from just her simple touch. He asked in a low voice, "How do you see today?"

"I'm sitting on the lap of the man I love. We're all alone, and I for one don't have anyplace urgent to go. The sun is shining so brightly the reflection on all that snow is almost blinding. We're warm and comfortable and dry. And alive. To me, it's truly a spectacular day."

There was a moment of thoughtful silence before Brent said, sounding much struck, "You're right. And I thank you for pointing it out to me." He nuzzled beneath her chin. "You really don't have to go to the shop?"

"Nope. Kallie works by herself today. I'll just call to check in later. And I'm considering hiring someone else as you suggested." She didn't add that she had decided to do that so she would have more time to spend with him. She had made enough declarations of her feelings without getting any in return.

Brent put his hand to her cheek, turning her to face him. "Will you spend the day with me? And the night? I rather liked the way you woke me this morning."

Shadow chuckled. "It was a little different from the way I woke you at my house, wasn't it?"

Brent nodded. "Morning screams are hell on my nervous system."

"I'll have to go home later to get a change of clothes and check my messages. Other than that, I'm all yours."

He stared at her mouth. "Hmm. I like the sound of that."

Shadow traced his huge grin with the tip of her finger. "Do you really want me to be all yours, Brent?"

Brent kissed her, a kiss filled with tenderness, but Shadow felt his hunger and need, too. He hadn't given her an answer, but she felt certain he cared for her, if just a little. He was smart to be cautious, especially with the way women had apparently feigned their affections, their real interest based on his financial standing.

It was beyond Shadow how any woman could be with Brent and not see the whole man—the strength, the intelligence, the innate compassion for other people. Thoughts of his money never entered her mind, except when he was trying to spend it on her, forcing her to object. But she understood his caution; Joan's visit had proved the necessity of that. That woman had plainly said she didn't mind sharing him with other women, as long as she was richly compensated. Shadow couldn't comprehend such a sentiment. If Brent went to another woman now, she'd want to scream, to maim and then cry, probably in that order. And she didn't think it was something she would ever be able to forgive him, for it would be such a break in trust. Just the thought made her shiver.

She snuggled closer to Brent, then laughed. "Your lap isn't quite as comfortable now as it was a minute ago. What happened?"

Brent said into her ear, his words gruff, "There's this incredibly soft, sexy woman sitting on me who keeps squirming around. She caused my libido to jump-start, and now it's in overdrive." He gently bit her earlobe, then licked the tender spot beneath her ear.

Shadow squirmed again. Her only comment to his outrageous teasing was, "Overdrive, huh? Oh good."

BRENT DIDN'T KNOW it was possible to have so much fun. Everything Shadow did, she did with pizzazz.

The electricity finally came back on that afternoon, and Shadow decided they should cook their own lunch. But she neglected to inform Brent she didn't know any more about cooking than he did, until it was too late. Making lasagna was a messy business. Shadow laughed her way through it, and even though the end result didn't look particularly appealing, it tasted perfect. Brent wasn't certain if that was due to the actual flavor of the dish or the fact that he shared it with Shadow.

She set up a picnic of sorts, using the same quilt they'd used the night before, spread before the fireplace, with lit candles all around and soft music in the background. She'd also insisted they eat naked. She said it greatly enhanced the flavor of the food. Later, she confessed hoping the sight of her nudity would distract Brent from what he ate, so he wouldn't actually notice what a poor job she'd done of it.

Later that day, after they had seen to having her car towed from the ditch, Shadow called in to Sex Appeal. Kallie had put a Help Wanted sign in the window, as per Shadow's instructions. Already there'd been several applications taken. It was while they were in his tub, enjoying a leisurely bath together, that Brent found out about her strange list of requirements for all applicants.

Shadow sat between his thighs, her back to his chest. Brent alternately rubbed his chin against the softness of her hair, breathed her scent and found various excuses to touch and stroke her. At the moment, he was washing her knee. "Why does the new assistant have to read a book in front of you?"

"Not just *any* book," Shadow clarified, "but a specific book that I've always found hilariously funny. If she reads it while I'm watching, and doesn't so much as crack a smile, or worse, if she actually frowns, I'll know she's not right for the job."

Brent ran a soapy hand over Shadow's shoulder. "What exactly is in this book?"

She leaned her head against his wet chest and looked at him upside down. "Slightly crude cartoons. Like the one with a couple lying under the covers in their bed, a multitude of, ah, sex toys scattered around them. The woman is looking at the poor guy, who has just emptied the entire box trying to spark her fancy, and she complains, 'I'm bored.'"

Brent smiled.

"There's also one where two businesswomen are talking over tea. One says, 'The only interesting man

I've met lately was an obscene phone caller, and he refused to give me his name no matter how I begged.'''

Idly cupping her breasts in his palms, Brent asked, "So if this unwary reader fails to laugh the appropriate number of times, you won't hire her?"

"That's right. But there are other deciding factors. Does she look pleasant or stern? And how she reacts to me. I can't have someone working for me who thinks I'm a certifiable nut. Not if she thinks being a nut is a bad thing."

Brent laughed, hugging Shadow to his chest. "You're priceless, honey, you know that? I've had so much fun today. Real fun. I think it's a first for me. Thank you."

"You're very welcome." She twisted in his arms, seeking a kiss. When the water cooled, Brent reluctantly moved her aside, then stood, quickly wrapping a towel around his waist.

Shadow, too, stepped out of the large tub, concerned by his withdrawal.

"Brent...?"

After slicking his wet hair off his forehead, he faced her. With his hands on his hips, not seeing any other way of broaching this, he said, "Stay here with me until this is all over."

She caught her breath. "Until *this* is over?"

"Until whoever is making those calls is either caught or goes away."

She shook her head. "I can't do that."

Though he'd half expected her refusal, it still annoyed him. "Why not? It's not like we haven't been intimate. And in this day and age, no one thinks anything of two people living together."

"I agreed to spend one night here, Brent. Not to

move in. Remember, I told you I come from an old-fashioned family. They'd be shocked if they found out I was living with a man."

"I want you safe, Shadow."

"I know," she replied gently. "And I appreciate your concern. But my house is safe, too. Judging by the cost of that dumb alarm system, it had better be secure."

Her attempt at humor went flat. "You think I'm only 'concerned' about you?" Brent gripped her bare shoulders, shaking her slightly. "I care about you, Shadow. Very much. It's a hell of a lot more than concern!"

She eyed him curiously, but said only, "What is it then, exactly?"

He released her with a muffled curse, turning away. Just as quickly he turned back. "Would you marry me if I asked?"

Her eyes rounded and her mouth opened twice before she managed to say, "If? You want to know before you actually ask?"

"Just answer the damn question," he growled.

She studied him in silence. "Why would you be asking?"

"What the hell do you mean, why?"

She tightened the towel around her waist, looking vulnerable. "You never said you love me. A proposal based on some noble sacrifice definitely wouldn't be acceptable."

Brent ground his teeth. "I'm not noble."

She nodded slowly. "Yes you are."

"I'm asking," he said succinctly, with flagging patience, "because I want you to marry me."

"But why?" She hugged herself tighter. "You're worried about me and you think marrying me is a way to keep me safe?"

There were a number of women who would have jumped at a proposal from him, and not one of them would have given him the third degree. They'd have said yes with alacrity and been thrilled. But not Shadow. No, she had to torture him a bit more by asking him questions he didn't have answers to.

Brent paced the floor, his hands fisted. Finally he turned to her again. "You could be pregnant," he reminded her.

She wasn't swayed. "So? I can take care of a baby. I may not have your wealth, but I can manage just fine. That would be a lousy reason to get married."

"You said you were old-fashioned," he accused with heat. "Children are a damn conventional reason to marry!"

"That's your only reason for asking? Suddenly, because I might be pregnant, you want to marry me?"

Brent floundered. Finally he took both her hands in his and led her to the bed. After she sat on the edge he started to speak again.

His eyes dropped to her exposed breasts, still damp from the bath. "I could do this a lot easier if you covered yourself properly."

She put one hand over each breast. "Now talk."

His groan turned into a laugh. "That doesn't help, honey. Your hands are too small to do an adequate job." He reached to the top of his large mahogany bed and jerked the pillow from beneath the spread. "Here. Hide yourself from me."

She covered herself, then gave him an expectant look.

"I care about you, Shadow. You know that." He waited until she nodded, then continued. "And after this morning, you could be pregnant."

He frowned pensively, adding, "I enjoy your company, which isn't something I can honestly say about any other woman I'm not related to, and even the relatives are few. Most of all, I don't like worrying about you. You can accuse me of being chauvinistic later, but I feel responsible for you and protective. So please," he asked quietly, "will you marry me?"

Sadness filled her eyes, making his heart almost stop. Then she smiled and leaned over to kiss him. Brent, wanting an answer, not a distraction, tried to pry her loose. But she fell against him and they both toppled to the floor. He landed with a thump, then groaned, but only until Shadow held his face between her hands and started kissing him.

Brent chuckled and finally managed to pull himself free enough to talk. "Does this mean yes or no?"

Shadow shoved away her towel, then his. Her fingers spread across his chest, tangling in his body hair. She straddled his hips and said, "No."

He froze, frustrated, angry. But Shadow was naked, astride his hips, and he was hard, ready. She rubbed against him, her eyes closed, her head tipped back, and he thought he'd shout with the pleasure of it.

"Shadow." He caught her hips and held her tighter to him.

"Where do you keep protection?"

She looked around the room until he said hoarsely, "In the nightstand." They'd talk later, he decided. He'd convince her then. Right now, he could barely breathe.

She curled her slender fingers around the base of his straining erection, stroked her thumb over the sensitive head, then did a tantalizing job of rolling on the condom. She held him steady and slowly lowered herself to slide down his length. He stiffened, his hips rising to meet her. She whispered breathlessly, all the while moving, "I'll never again marry a man who doesn't love me. For any reason."

Brent raised his hands to her breasts, urging her on, his fingers finding and toying with her nipples, plucking, tugging, rolling them gently. Shadow arched her back and her thighs tightened. At the moment of her release, she again shouted that she loved him, then collapsed against his chest. He came with his own deep groan of fulfillment.

Long after the waves of her climax had receded, Shadow was still kissing him, though gently now, tender little nips on his chin and throat. She said again, "I love you, Brent."

Brent sighed, his hands holding her close in near desperation for just a moment. "What am I going to do with you, Shadow?"

She propped her elbows on his chest and stared down at him. "Do with me? You mean more than you've already done? I didn't know there was more, but hey, I'm all for it."

He smiled, but it was only a halfhearted effort.

Shadow leaned back down and cuddled against him. "We can simply continue as we are. Having fun. Enjoying each other. Making the most of our time together."

"I don't like the sound of that," he warned, eyeing her closely. "As if our time is limited."

"Well..." She toyed with the lock of hair over his forehead, before meeting his gaze. "I don't plan to go anywhere. But I wouldn't want you to stay here if you were unhappy."

"How could I be unhappy with you around?"

Brent could tell by her remote shrug that he'd hurt

her. He wanted to kick his own ass, but more than that, he wanted to see her smile again, to hear her laugh. Her laughter never failed to arouse him and her smiles made him feel like the luckiest man alive.

He could tell her he loved her, he thought, whether he was certain of his feelings or not. But Shadow was always honest with him and she deserved his honesty in return.

He cared, just as he'd told her. But he didn't know about love; it wasn't something tangible, wasn't something he could easily grasp. Shadow was unique and different and…special. The way she made him feel was special. She said she loved him.

But, a tiny voice in his head insisted, *plenty of women have claimed to love you.*

Shadow shoved herself up into a sitting position. She brushed her hair out of her eyes. "I need to go home, Brent. I have to check my messages and—"

"You're coming back here tonight, Shadow." He had no intention of letting anyone, especially some loony secret admirer, get near her. She wouldn't be hurt. He'd see to that, one way or another.

"Don't get all heavy-handed and bossy on me, Brent. I said I would spend the night. But I need some clothes and my makeup and a few other things. Tomorrow is a workday, and I'll probably go straight from here."

"All right." Brent lifted them both to their feet. He couldn't keep his eyes, or his hands, off Shadow's naked body, with her standing so sweetly before him. He touched her cheek, her kiss-swollen lips. "Will you try to hire someone tomorrow? I don't want you working alone anymore." She started to draw back, ready to refuse, and he teased, "I did ask nicely that time. No demands at all. You see, I'm trying, even though I personally think I'm much better at issuing orders." He grinned at her. "Ah, the concessions I make for you."

"True." She chuckled, then gave up with a groan. "I'll see if there isn't a worthy applicant in the bunch first thing tomorrow morning. How's that?"

"It's great." Then he added, "For now."

8

STILL HEARING THE ECHO of the last message to play, Shadow stared at her answering machine. He'd called her again, not once, not twice, but *three times*. And he hadn't been happy. No, he'd been nearly incoherent with jealousy and anger.

She rubbed her arms and looked at Brent.

"This changes everything," Brent said, and his voice was as hard as his expression.

What could she say? "I...I don't know."

Brent nodded, then started for her bedroom.

"Where are you going?"

He didn't look at her. "To pack some of your clothes."

She hustled after him. "I can do that." Though she'd never admit it to Brent, she was relieved she wouldn't be staying home alone tonight. "I'll only need a few things for tomorrow."

Brent ignored her, rummaging through her closet until he found a suitcase, then opening it on her bed.

"Brent, I don't need that case. I'll only...wait a minute! Brent, *stop*." She caught his hand, now in possession of two shirts. "What do you think you're doing?"

"You're not staying here alone."

She didn't want to, but she heard herself say, in a firm voice, "You can't force me to stay at your house."

He leaned down, eyes narrowed, and said through his teeth, "Watch me."

"I don't believe this!" Her nervousness over the calls was forgotten, smothered beneath her need for independence.

He stepped past her. "What's your parents' phone number?"

Shadow watched him suspiciously. She'd seen many moods from him, but this was a new one. "Now, Brent..."

He stalked to her little telephone table by the front door, opened a drawer and riffled through it until he located her personal phone book. Intent on his purpose, he paid no mind to Shadow's escalating temper.

She practically shouted, "I don't have my parents' number written down! Good grief, I know it by heart. It hasn't changed since I was ten years old."

Brent faced her. "Tell it to me."

This was interesting. She folded her arms over her chest, wondering what Brent intended to say to her parents. She'd told them a little about him, but nothing at all about the anonymous calls. Deciding quickly, she recited the number.

He dialed it without hesitation.

"Hello, Mrs. Callahan? This is Brent Bramwell, a friend of Shadow's." He paused, then said, "Oh, she told you about me?" His gaze met Shadow's briefly and she could have sworn that was raw satisfaction dancing in his dark green eyes. "She's fine, ma'am. No, I swear, nothing's wrong with her. That is, nothing you aren't already aware of. Yes, of course I was joking."

Shadow stuck her tongue out at him. He covered the mouthpiece and whispered, "Not yet, honey. How about when we get to my house?"

Her face colored, which only satisfied him more.

Brent listened a few minutes, laughed a few times, then explained about the calls, the flowers, the notes. He was very detailed, Shadow thought, peeved. But he was also calm enough that he wouldn't alarm her mother. He surprised Shadow by telling her mother that he wanted Shadow to stay with him.

"Yes, ma'am, but the thing is, she's concerned she'll shock you. I understand, but she'll be much safer with me until this whole thing can be resolved. I thought you might be able to talk some sense into her."

Brent's gaze filled with triumph and he handed her the phone. His grin was entirely too smug.

Shadow, knowing her mother well, took the phone and said without preamble, "No, Mom, I won't come home. I know, but I'm fine, really. No, it's true. I have this outrageously expensive security system Brent insisted on me buying...." She paused, then said, "Yeah, I suppose he is. I'm not sure about that. He hasn't really said. Yes, I love him."

Shadow could tell by the look on Brent's face that this wasn't the conversation he'd anticipated. Rather than her mother telling her to go with Brent, she was trying to coerce her into coming home. Shadow could have told Brent what the outcome of his call would be.

She rolled her eyes. "All right, Mom, I'll think about it. Give my love to everyone." She laughed. "Right. Goodbye."

Brent scowled at her. "What in hell was that all about?"

"My mother said you sound like a rascal and a thoroughly likable young man. She also said I should try to keep you happy so you'd stick around."

"What did she say about you staying with me?"

"When she accepted that I wouldn't come home, she said that I probably should and to be very careful if I don't."

"Aha! So she agrees with me?"

Shadow shrugged again, barely managing to hold her laughter. "I suppose she did. But, Brent, I'm thirty-one. I don't always do what my parents want me to. I told you before, I've been on my own since I was seventeen."

"Does that mean you will or won't stay with me?" he demanded.

"Tonight I'll stay. Tomorrow I have to be at my own house." His anger and frustration were palpable and Shadow went to him, gently touching his arm. "Brent, can't you understand?"

"That you want to drive me nuts? Oh yeah, I understand that well enough."

"If I come to stay with you, it will mean I let him drive me out of my house. I'd be miserable knowing I'd given up."

"I wouldn't let you be miserable."

He was such an easy man to love, she thought with a small chuckle. "We both have jobs to go to, other commitments." He didn't relent, and she added, "Would you leave your home because of a few phone calls?"

He snorted at that, then turned thoughtful. "All right," he said finally. "But remember, I did give you options."

Shadow was surprised and perversely disappointed by how quickly he gave up. She turned away to finish her packing.

It was already dark outside, even though it wasn't quite seven. Brent stood by her side as she turned on the security system, then walked out to his car. He held her small overnight bag in one hand, her arm with the other. She was silent on the drive to his house, feeling melancholy again, a mood she wasn't familiar with and didn't quite know how to handle.

They entered Brent's house to the sound of a ringing phone. Brent had headed for the bedroom, so Shadow picked it up. She listened for only a moment, not saying a word after her initial greeting. Brent sauntered back in, and she handed him the phone with a wry smile. "It's your stalker, not mine."

"What?" Brent took the receiver with a curt, "Hello?" Then he groaned. "What do you want, Joan?"

Wanting to give him privacy, Shadow wandered aimlessly through the house. It was beautiful, but not decorated to its full potential. With diamond-paned windows, hardwood floors and a fireplace in nearly every room, the place bordered on historic, but the spacious rooms were largely empty, the walls bare. The few pieces of furniture or rugs were purely functional, not at all decorative. The only completed rooms in the entire massive, five-bedroom house were the family room, the kitchen and Brent's bedroom. These were furnished with heavy mahogany and cherry-wood pieces done in bold, basic designs. There wasn't a plant or a picture to be found.

Shadow was looking at a guest bedroom, one close to the hall bath, when Brent found her. She'd been thinking what a wonderful room it would be for a child. Overlooking the backyard, it had a closet big enough to be a play space, filled with plenty of shelves for toys.

She turned to Brent, trying to mask her thoughts. "Did you get everything straightened out with Joan?"

"She wanted me to have dinner with her."

"You told her no?"

"Of course I told her no. I have no interest in seeing her again. I wish to hell she'd leave me alone."

Shadow smiled. "She told me yesterday that you were unfaithful to her during your engagement."

Brent stiffened. "What did you say?"

"Not much. Mostly I just listened. I decided she was lying." Shadow looked down at her hands, clasped in Brent's much larger ones. "She's not a happy woman, Brent."

He rubbed her knuckles and asked, "Why do you say that?"

"Because she doesn't understand what will make her happy. She thinks you and your money will do it for her. She doesn't know she has to make herself happy, not rely on someone else to do it for her."

Brent frowned at her. "What're you trying to tell me in your twisted way, Shadow?"

She asked suddenly, "You haven't done much with this house. Why is that?"

He searched her face. "Your quick turns in conversation make me dizzy. All right. I haven't done much here because I wasn't certain I'd stay, and I haven't had a lot of free time."

"Are you certain now?"

Borrowing her tactics, he didn't answer but asked his own question instead. "What's this all about, honey?"

"My mother asked me if you planned to stay in town or if this was a temporary visit to take care of business. I didn't know the answer to that. It made me realize there's a lot I don't know about you. What your plans are for the future, what you want say...five years from now. If you've set any long-term goals for yourself. I was just curious, I suppose."

Brent chewed on the inside of his cheek, scrutinizing her. "And you decided to ask all these questions here, in this particular bedroom? Or was it because of Joan's call?"

Shadow shook her head.

"I don't understand you, Shadow. Nothing new in that, I suppose. But I've asked you to marry me and that alone should tell you I don't plan to uproot anytime soon. Or even if I had planned to, I wouldn't go unless you could go, too. And as far as my goals for the future, I haven't set any. My business ventures are forever expanding, so I don't have to consciously set goals for them. I simply grow and expand with them."

"And personal goals? Any thoughts on them?"

"Only to the point that I'm thirty-four and therefore at an age where I should be having children of my own, a wife to come home to." He lifted her hand to his chest. "We could have a very nice life together, Shadow."

It wouldn't be enough, she knew, not without his love. But she couldn't tell him that. She'd made too many demands already. "Don't you see? We could have a nice life apart, too. You shouldn't consider marriage just because it'd be convenient right now."

He placed his palm over her flat belly. "And if you're pregnant? That would be a lifetime commitment for both of us."

"You wouldn't have to be married to me to do your duty to the child."

Brent thrust his hands in his pockets and turned away. "It wouldn't be a matter of duty." He whirled back to face her. "Do you think I'd avoid involvement in my child's life?"

Helplessly, she stared at him. "I don't know, that's just it. I mean, there's involved, and then there's *involved*." She smiled, trying to lighten the tension in the room. "This may all be a moot point. The odds of me being pregnant can't be all that great."

"Oh, I don't know. Not to brag, but I'm good at anything I do." He touched her belly again and looked almost wistful. "I'd say it's possible."

"But not probable. Let's wait before we worry that topic into the ground, okay?"

Brent gave long consideration to her suggestion and finally nodded. Shadow had the distinct impression he'd made a strategic—and temporary—retreat. "What would you like to do for dinner? We haven't eaten yet."

"Do you have peanut butter and jelly?"

"Uh, no. I don't think so."

"Then the first order of business is a trip to the grocery. Then—" she yawned dramatically "—I think I'd like to make an early night of it. What do you say?"

"Do you intend to attack me again?"

"I was considering it."

Brent instantly feigned his own yawn, complete with an elaborate stretch. "I suddenly feel faint with exhaustion. An early night it is."

SHE GOT ANOTHER CALL the next day. Shadow's temper was frayed to the limit, her disposition not to be envied, and she hadn't gotten enough sleep the night before. The only bad thing about that was it couldn't be blamed on Brent. They'd made love twice, then he'd fallen asleep, his arms around her, her head on his shoulder. It was the most comfortable position imaginable, yet sleeplessness had kept her up long into the night.

The call was short, something about showing her who was in control. Ha! She already knew—Brent was.

Without trying, he'd managed to control her thoughts, her feelings. Effortlessly, he made her want him, love him...*almost* need him. Life had taught her to need no one but herself.

Her life would be every bit as complete without him.

Who was she kidding? Brent was the part of her she hadn't known was missing, a part that filled her up, made her whole, more content, more fulfilled. She could make it without him—she wasn't dramatic or a fatalist. Life wouldn't end without Brent. But it sure wouldn't be as wonderful, either. Not even close.

Shadow paced, ignoring the pile of papers on her desk that needed her attention, knowing she should be out front helping train the new girl she'd hired just that morning. But she couldn't seem to clear her mind. The papers would wait and Kallie did a commendable job of training. When the phone rang, Shadow stared at it, a malicious smile slowly dawning over her face. She needed an outlet for her temper and her annoying admirer would do just fine.

"Hello?" she fairly sang.

"I wanted to give you fair warning."

Oh, hell. Wrong stalker. "What do you want, Joan?"

"I told you. Just a friendly little warning. Brent will tire of you soon. Then I'll have him back. Why don't you save yourself a little heartache and give up?"

"Well, now," Shadow said, her voice sugary sweet with politeness, "I appreciate your concern for my welfare, indeed I do. But it's unnecessary. Truly. You see,

I'm enjoying every little minute I spend with Brent. So no matter how long it lasts, there won't be a single wasted second."

"You little bitch! Can't you see he's only using you?"

"That's okay. I'm using him, too." Shadow could hear Joan gnashing her teeth. It pleased her.

"I'm going to see him this afternoon. He likes to make love in his office, did you know that?"

Her words had been softer, more in control. Shadow grimaced, not liking the mental picture that formed. She said carefully, "I had the impression Brent liked making love just about anywhere. But no, I haven't been to his office."

"Well, I have. I *will* get him back."

Rapidly tiring of the game, Shadow said, "Joan, if you can get him back, then I don't want him anyway. I wish you luck." And she hung up. *Spiteful witch*. She thought about calling Brent and warning him, then decided it might smack of jealousy, so she resumed her pacing instead.

Ten minutes later, she got yet another call and this one was from her number one annoyance. Shadow thought, rather humorlessly, that he must be as bored as she was, but most probably for different reasons. She already missed Brent terribly. This guy was just plain *missing*.

"What do you want now?" she asked.

"Are you going to spend the night with him again?"

She didn't bother asking which "him" he meant. "That's really none of your business and if you don't stop pestering me I'm going to have my calls traced."

He yelled, "You stay away from that businessman and I won't have to call!"

"Everyone seems to want to issue warnings to me today."

He was thrown by her words. "What's that supposed to mean?"

"Never mind. Inside joke. But tell me. I have been wondering and since you seem determined to keep calling, we may as well talk." She felt smug at the thought of his silent confusion. "How did you get Brent's phone number?"

"I saw the two of you together," he accused.

"Where?"

"At the shop, at your house."

His answers were smooth. Too smooth. And suspiciously smug. "So how did you know who he was?"

"I followed him back to his office. Once I knew his name, I looked up his number in the phone book."

Shadow felt a chill, but concealed it behind her cool manner. She was only just realizing that any threat to her extended to Brent as well. Maybe more so. "Why are you doing this? Why me? Was it something I said," she asked carefully, "when you entered the contest?"

He laughed. "I have no idea what you're talking about."

"That doesn't surprise me."

She actually felt his anger as he blustered into the phone. "He doesn't love you, you know. He won't be around forever. You can keep throwing yourself at him, keep chasing him, but it won't do you any good!"

Shadow hung up, his words too closely resembling her own thoughts and Joan's warning. She opened a file drawer and pulled out the phone book. Quickly flipping through the pages, she stopped at the Bs. Brent's name wasn't listed; he hadn't been in town long enough. How had this nut gotten the number?

Had he, at some point, been close enough to listen to one of their conversations? Shadow envisioned him hiding behind a bush, concealed by the heavy snow and the early winter darkness. She and Brent had had several talks on the walkway, both in front of her house and at the shop. It sent shivers down her spine to think of someone watching and listening so intently.

She couldn't let it affect her like this, making her paranoid. She forced herself to take a deep breath, to calm down. The police had told her that lots of people got strange calls. Usually it turned out to be nothing. She had taken precautions; he couldn't touch her, if that was even his plan.

She put on her coat and walked to the coffee shop. She was skittish, and as she walked, even in the light of day, she found herself looking all around, being overly cautious. It irritated her.

There were several friends at the coffee shop, different proprietors of the various businesses. The big talk over coffee was how the contest was faring. Shadow hadn't met the two men Brent sent to fill her quota. But the women were very enthusiastic about them. The men were described as successful, handsome and charming. The photographer was more than ready to brag that she had a date lined up with one of them already.

That sounded just a tad unethical to Shadow, but she didn't say so. After all, the shoppers would make the ultimate decision on the winner, not the shop owners.

When Shadow returned to her office, she called her mom. Thanksgiving was just around the corner so she made a last-minute check on what, if anything, she should bring. All that was required was herself. She dragged the conversation out for a good fifteen minutes, trying to distract herself from her worries, but she finally ran out of gossip and was forced to hang up.

She hesitated a few minutes, at loose ends as to what to do next. It was a given that she wouldn't accomplish any work. After a brief struggle with herself, she gave in and called Brent. His secretary, a very pleasant woman, announced he was busy in his office and not to be disturbed.

His office. The question came out without her mind's permission. "Is he with Joan?"

The secretary, Micky, was clearly surprised as she answered. "Yes, he's with Miss Howard. Were they expecting you?"

It took Shadow a moment to reply because she had to find a way to keep the screech out of her tone. Finally she said, "Nope. They're not expecting me."

"Oh. Well then, can I take a message?"

"Yes. Tell Brent, er, Mr. Bramwell, that I went home for the day."

"Yes, ma'am. And what is your name again?"

Shadow hung up without answering. Brent would know who the message was from. There was no need for her name to be announced to the secretary or possibly in front of Joan.

She didn't want to indulge in wicked imaginings, but her mind refused to listen to her, conjuring visions of Brent and Joan together. Shadow had never been jealous a day in her life. It had always been a foreign emotion to her, something other people suffered through insecurities and indecision. Her attitude had always been that if a man wasn't trustworthy you got rid of him.

Of course, she reminded herself, Brent was trustworthy. It was that she-devil Joan who couldn't be trusted.

Brent was probably doing everything possible to put her off. Did he truly loathe Joan as he said, or was it possible she might seduce him?

Thoroughly disgusted with herself, Shadow threw on her coat and went out to the sales floor to announce to Kallie that she was leaving. Kallie looked at her with concern. "Are you all right? You look a little down."

Shadow laughed. "You're shocked by such a notion, Kallie?"

"Well, you're always so chipper. I don't remember ever seeing you looking quite so...glum."

"I think I've just been fed a good dose of reality, that's all. I'm sure I'll recover. But I am tired and I'm not doing a single constructive thing around here, so I might as well get out of your way."

"You be careful going home."

"I will. And you be careful locking up. Make certain you're not alone in the parking lot at night. Now that we have another helper, we should always leave here in twos."

Kallie agreed, then gave Shadow a hug. "Get a good night's sleep and I'll see you in the morning."

Shadow drove home by rote. Even the freezing chill of the air didn't faze her.

The sight of her house did, however. Shadow finally thought of something to do that would take her mind off Brent. She went in, using the remote control device so her alarm wouldn't sound, then turned off the system. She would be running in and out and didn't want to be bothered using the remote each time.

She changed into her oldest jeans and a baggy, well-worn sweatshirt that read Talk Is Cheap (But the Action Will Cost Ya'). She spent the next half hour shoveling snow off her porch and walk. It felt good to do physical work instead of sitting in her office; the exercise helped clear her mind. The day was so cold, not a single neighbor ventured outside and no cars drove by.

When she'd finished, she went inside and made herself a sandwich, with a glass of juice and two cookies for lunch. She sat at the table, pensive as she waited for Brent to phone. There was no doubt he would call. It was only a matter of when he finished with Joan.

She cringed at her own mental wording. Downing the last of the juice, she stood to leave the kitchen. She needed a hot shower to warm herself.

Outside, the wind blew, chasing snowflakes past the windows, rustling the trees, forming drifts around the yard. She heard the occasional creak and snap as the house settled. She realized how alone she was; she'd never felt lonely before, but now, without Brent, she did.

She recalled the security system, which she hadn't turned back on. She barely got it reset when her head started to swim. She stopped, flattening one hand on the wall. Her stomach pitched, churned. She forced herself to breathe slowly, but a heavy lethargy was settling in. It was just like the night she'd spent with Brent. She barely made it to the bathroom on time. Her stomach was completely empty before she could finally leave the toilet.

Wondering if she had the flu, she walked slowly into her bedroom and stripped off her clothes. After pulling on a short, thermal nightgown, she crawled beneath the covers and tried to find a comfortable position. She was about to doze off when the phone began ringing.

She thought, *please, not again.* Groaning, she leaned out of bed and picked up the receiver on the nightstand. Her voice was a hesitant croak. "Hello?"

"Why did you leave the shop without telling me first?" he demanded.

Shadow hung up on him. The last thing she wanted was to have Brent yelling at her.

He called back immediately. She picked up the receiver and he said, his voice low and mean, "I wouldn't suggest you do that again."

Shadow waited. Brent said, now more cautiously, "Shadow?"

"What?"

"Are you all right?"

"Yes. No, actually, I'm sick."

Trying for a more moderate tone, he asked, "Then why didn't you tell my secretary that when you called? You know I don't want you driving home alone."

"You were with Joan. I was having my first major bout of jealousy. I didn't want or need to get your approval to go home. And besides, I just got sick. I wasn't sick when I left."

There was a moment of silence while Brent digested everything she had just said. Without addressing any one issue, he said, "I'll be there in just a minute, honey."

"I might be catching," she said, thinking of the flu. This time he hung up on her. Shadow put her head under the pillow. It seemed like only minutes later that Brent was pounding on the front door.

"Wow. You look like hell. Are you okay?"

She glared at him. "Thanks, Brent. I needed to hear that."

Brent grinned at her disgruntled frown, watching as she walked, hunched over like an old woman, back to bed. He followed behind her. "What's the matter, honey?"

"I got really tired again and then sick to my stomach. Just out of the blue—ugh. I hate throwing up."

"Well, I can understand that." Brent helped her into the bed and under the covers, then he felt her head. "You don't have a fever. Did you eat anything bad?"

She shot him a venomous look through shadowed eyes. "If I knew it was bad, would I have eaten it?"

"Okay." He pursed his mouth to keep from grinning. She was so testy when she didn't feel well. "What *have* you eaten today?"

"Breakfast with you this morning. Then a sandwich and a couple of cookies just a little bit ago. That's all."

"What kind of sandwich?"

"Peanut butter. And no. The peanut butter wasn't bad."

Brent frowned. "I'm going to call the doctor."

"No, Brent, that's silly. I'm fine. I'm already starting to feel better. Not so weak."

Brent stared at her thoughtfully, his mind churning over possibilities. "What did you drink with your lunch?"

"Just some fruit juice."

"Is there any left?"

"In the fridge."

He stood. "I'm going to dump it just in case it's bad. I'll also make you a cup of hot tea. Does that sound good?"

Shadow nodded. "It's odd. But I feel almost hungry again."

"Do you have any canned soup I could warm up for you?"

She curled a fist under her pale cheek, looking be-

yond pathetic, then mumbled, "I don't want you waiting on me."

Her stubbornness passed all bounds. He said without a hint of a smile, "I'm still annoyed with you,
sweetheart. Don't press your luck."

"All right!" she said, flopping onto her back and
then groaning from the sudden movement. She put her
hands over her eyes. "Make the damned soup. You can
feed it to me, too, if you want. After all, I'm completely
helpless, right? That is why you're angry? Because I
did the unthinkable and came home on my own, actually driving myself! Why, it's unheard of! Scandalous!"

Brent retained his stern expression all through her
theatrics. When she quieted, holding her belly and
squinting in pain, he asked, "Are you through? Good.
Now, I think I'll fix the soup, which you will feed to
yourself, then you and I are going to straighten a few
things out."

"You're not my boss, Brent Bramwell!" she called after him. "Why do I have to keep reminding you of
that?" He didn't answer, and she added very quietly,
for her own benefit, "You're not even my husband."

But Brent heard. "I will be," he stated firmly, loud
and clear. "I've made up my mind, Shadow. And
there's no way you're going to change it now."

9

"ARE YOU DONE SULKING?"

Shadow flashed him a narrow-eyed look filled with promised retribution. Brent only raised his left brow, waiting.

She set her soup bowl, now empty, on the nightstand. "I never before sulked in my life. I was never melancholy and I never, positively *never* suffered jealousy. There are definite side effects to loving you, Brent Bramwell. Unpleasant ones."

He grinned at her. "Then we're even. You've made me face up to a few unfamiliar feelings, too. Believe it or not, I've never been so protective, though the women I've known wanted someone to take care of them, to make their lives easier. You, on the other hand, are too open and friendly for your own good. You scare me to death."

"Scare you?" Shadow asked blankly.

"That's right. And fear is another emotion I'm not exactly used to dealing with. And possessiveness and this damned tenderness that nearly chokes me. On top of all that, I'm forever losing control around you, one way or another."

Shadow fiddled with the edge of the blanket, running the silken hem between her fingers. "Are we hopeless, then, do you think? Are you saying it's not worth it?"

Brent leaned forward intently until their noses nearly touched. "I'm not saying anything of the kind." He kissed the tip of her chin. "You expect me to label what I'm feeling, Shadow. But I've never felt it before, so how can I? I understand that you're impatient. You're filled with energy and excitement. You want to do everything now, right this minute. But I'm not that way. Believe it or not, I'm generally concise and controlled. Everything I do is well thought out and planned. But you have me jumping through hoops, making an ass of myself with great regularity. As far as carefully planning anything, I haven't had a peaceful moment to do that since I met you."

"It hasn't been very conventional, has it?" she asked. "Our time together, I mean. What with the phone calls, and then Joan showing up." She was silent a moment. "Have I really been rushing you so much?"

Brent laughed, chucking her chin. "You rush everything and everybody, honey. It's part of your personality. I've never known anyone whose mind worked so quickly, always changing directions, leaving me and everyone else in your dust."

She laughed. "Stop it, Brent. I'm not that bad."

"You're not bad at all. You're wonderful. And I'm enjoying every minute with you, chaotic as it may be. I want you to remember that, okay?" He rose to stand beside the bed. "Now, are you feeling better?" At her nod, he said, "Good. We have other things to talk about."

"You're back to sounding stern, Brent."

"I'm feeling particularly stern, too. It was foolish of you to leave the shop alone today. And don't think I didn't notice that you shoveled the walk. You left yourself out in the open, vulnerable, and all because you gave in to some completely unfounded and ridiculous notion of jealousy. I told you I didn't care a thing about Joan. I thought you trusted me. I thought you believed me."

Shadow stiffened dangerously. "Are you through?"

"No, I'm not. I feel like turning you over my knee."

"I'd like to see you try it." She looked mutinous, murderous, all one hundred twenty pounds of her. He bit back his pleased smile. God, he enjoyed her gumption.

"You scared me spitless, for no good reason. You acted selfishly, not caring how I might feel when I found out you'd gone home alone, how rejected I might feel."

She snorted at that obvious nonsense. Brent ignored her.

"I understand, what with your history with men, why you want to be independent. I respect that, too, because I know I wouldn't want to be dependent on anyone else. But sweetheart, there's such a thing as being too independent. Since I've decided we will marry—no, don't shake your head, I'm confident I'll be able to wear you down—"

"Ha! Not by acting like an autocratic jerk."

"—I'm going to move in."

Shadow could only stare. *"What?"*

"You heard me. You won't come to my house, so I'm coming to yours. You're putting me through hell with your contrariness, and I can't take it anymore." He stared down at her, not blinking, then said again, "I gave you the option of moving in with me. You turned me down, so I'm moving in with you."

"No."

"Afraid so. If you don't want to sleep with me, I'll

camp out on the couch. Or I'll open one of your rooms upstairs. But I'm going to be close so I'll know nothing can happen to you."

"My couch is too short for you and I told you those rooms upstairs haven't been touched since I bought the place. They're not even furnished."

His expression was wry. "I can afford to buy a damn bed."

"They're cold! You wouldn't be comfortable there."

"I'm sure as hell not comfortable sitting at home and worrying either." He added more softly, "I don't like to worry, Shadow. It's not something I've had much practice with. I don't think I do it particularly well. So I'm moving in."

It took Shadow a minute of silent consideration and then she grinned, totally confounding Brent. But that was okay, he was used to it by now.

"All right. You can stay here."

Brent hadn't realized how tense he'd been until she said that. He relaxed, letting out a held breath. His fists uncurled, opening as he smoothed his palms up and down his thighs. He realized she was watching him with a calculated gleam in her honey-colored eyes, and he nearly grimaced. Was a man ever in such desperate straits? And even more important, would he ever feel like himself again? His old self, the one he knew so well?

With forced aplomb, he managed a cocky grin and said to Shadow, "All right then. I'll go grab a few things and be back in under an hour. If you're up to it, why don't you make a grocery list for me? I want to buy some bottled water, anyway. It could be your cistern is contaminated, or the pipes in a house this old might be causing a water problem. That could be why you've been ill."

Shadow smiled complacently at him and started to leave the bed. Brent stopped her. "I don't like these strange illnesses that keep hitting you. I'll get you a pen and paper and you make the list right here."

"I feel fine now, Brent, you don't have to coddle me."

Exasperated, he growled, "I'll damn well coddle you if it pleases me to do so!"

His outburst brought her a fat smile. He threw up his hands and left the room to locate the paper and pen.

When he returned, Shadow was sitting cross-legged in the center of the bed. She said, "All right. I'll write down a few necessities and you can explain to me what you were doing in your office with Joan."

"Doing? I wasn't doing anything with her. We talked." Brent handed her the pen and paper.

Shadow wrote a few items on the list, then asked, "About what?"

"You're not still jealous, are you? There's really no reason, honey."

"No. I believe you. But I'm still curious. She called me earlier today." Shadow peeked up at him. "She informed me that you like to make love in your office and that she was going to see you. She also made some general insults. Nothing new."

Brent flushed. "I didn't touch her."

"I didn't really think you would."

At least she trusted him that much, Brent thought. "I considered what you told me. About each person finding his own happiness. When Joan tried to resurrect the past, I asked her how much money would make her happy enough to leave me alone."

Shadow gaped. "You didn't!"

"Yes I did. She slapped me, then screeched for a minute or two, looking frankly insulted, and finally demanded I apologize." Brent smiled at Shadow's enthralled interest. "I did. And then we talked, probably for the first time. Before she left, she offered to give me back the bracelet."

Shadow waited, her eyes wide.

"I insisted she keep it. As a sort of farewell gift."

Shadow scampered from the bed and threw her arms around him. "You really are a nice guy, you know that?"

"Then you're not mad anymore?"

Shadow kissed him. "Of course not. I'm glad you were kind to her."

"And you'll quit complaining when I want to coddle you?"

"We'll deal with that on an as-it-comes basis."

Smoothing down her unruly curls, Brent hugged her, his eyes filled with tenderness. "You're incredible." She lowered her gaze, toying with his shirt buttons.

Feelings swamped him—overwhelming, invading feelings—and he shook his head to clear it. "Did your swain call again?"

"That's right! I meant to tell you. He said he got your phone number from the book. But you're not listed."

"If he knew my name, he could have called information."

"I suppose. But he said other things. It almost sounded like he'd overheard us talking." She shivered. "It gives me the creeps to think about him being close enough to listen in on our conversations."

"He won't get close to you again. I promise."

"My hero," she teased. "Brent, it's not your responsibility to make that promise."

"I'm not about to let anyone hurt you, whether you think it's my responsibility or not." The idea of anyone threatening her did more than give him the creeps; it filled him with rage and scared the hell out of him. He had a gut feeling about all this. And until that feeling went away, he planned to stay close to Shadow's side, guarding her whether she thought she needed him or not.

They went over the grocery list together, a domestic chore they both enjoyed. Of course, anything Shadow did she did with laughter and teasing and pleasure. And Shadow was so openly sexual, so honest in her enjoyment of Brent, she didn't think twice about suggesting he add condoms to the bottom of the list.

Relieved that he wouldn't have to sleep on the couch, or renovate her vacant upstairs, Brent promised to pick up an adequate supply.

He left Shadow lying drowsily in her bed, looking so soft and feminine and desirable he wished he'd already gone and was on his way home. He kissed her gently on the forehead, listened to her whispered words of love and left with his mind a jumble of emotions, some so sweet they made his teeth ache, others so all encompassing he found it hard to draw a breath.

"DO YOU HAVE TO WORK LATE today?"

Brent smiled at Shadow over his morning coffee. "I can get off anytime. Why? You got something special in mind?"

Appearing vaguely shy, Shadow replied, "No. I took the day off. I was just thinking we could watch a movie and maybe pop some corn. I think I could even do dinner if you're interested."

She was nervous, uncertain how they should proceed, Brent realized. It had been a long time since she'd had anyone live, even temporarily, in a house with her. Checking his watch, Brent calculated quickly in his mind, then said, "I can be home by four. Will that do?"

Shadow beamed at him. "That would be perfect. I have laundry and a little cleaning to do before then, anyway."

"Don't overdo it, sweetheart. If you're still not feeling well..."

"Oh, I feel fine now. Just a little tired, is all. But I did hire an extra girl for the shop and she's anxious for the hours. Kallie said she's doing fine, so there's really no reason for me to go in. Besides, the weather looks nasty again. And they're predicting a record low today. I just thought it would be nicer to stay home for a change."

Brent searched her face. "If I didn't have a board meeting, I'd cancel my appointments...."

"Don't be silly. I'm fine. Really."

He could tell she wasn't fine. She was nervous, probably thinking about the phone calls and how close someone had gotten to her. Brent felt the now familiar rage, but squelched it. It wouldn't do to frighten her further.

He finished his coffee, stood to put his cup in the sink, then went to Shadow, pulling her from her seat. "Give me a hug and a kiss that will last me until I get home."

Home. That sounded very nice to Brent. Shadow squeezed him fiercely, almost desperately, then curled his toes with a passion packed, tongue licking kiss. She nearly fried his eyeballs with her enthusiasm. "Be careful, Brent. The roads are icy and too many people drive like idiots in the snow."

"I will. And Shadow?"

"Hmm?"

"It was very nice waking up with you beside me this morning."

"Especially since there weren't any screams?" she teased.

"It would have been nice even with a scream." He sought words to explain to her how much it meant to him, exactly how nice it had been, but came up blank. She gave her love so freely, but it wasn't that easy for him. He wasn't now and never had been a free spirit. His businesses, his life, his background all had required iron control.

He settled on saying simply, "Thank you."

Her smile warmed and her gaze lazily caressed his face. "You're very welcome. It was my pleasure." She touched his jaw. "I like waking with you, too, Brent. You're very handsome with your hair on end and whiskers covering your face. Your eyes are so dark in the morning, very sexy. Bedroom eyes."

Brent groaned. "Keep that up and I'll never get out of here." He kissed her again, quick and hard, then grabbed his coat. "Set the alarm as soon as I'm out the door."

"Quit worrying. I'll be fine."

"We already established my right to worry if I feel like it." He opened the door, then turned to her. "Be good," he said.

Shadow gave an exasperated laugh. Closing the door after him, she said to herself, "I'm not certain you'd enjoy me quite as much, Mr. Bramwell, if I actually behaved myself." She had a lot to do before Brent got home…. Home. The sound of that sent a thrill down her spine. She headed off for the laundry room, whistling happily.

SHE'D BEEN RIGHT to let him move in, Shadow decided a few days later. Once she'd thought about it, it had made sense. If he didn't love her yet, familiarity might take care of that. And in the meantime, she had him all to herself.

They'd settled into a domestic routine. The weather turned abominable, but even that suited Shadow just fine. Outside of work, they spent all their time together and were learning more about each other with every passing day.

They missed Thanksgiving. With temperatures dropping to fifteen below, the windchill was at a dangerous level. Rather than brave the cold evening, they opted for their own private dinner.

There were no more phone calls, and more important, Shadow became increasingly positive she was pregnant.

Brent hadn't asked, so she hadn't yet volunteered the information, preferring to make certain with a medical exam before telling him. But as each day went by, she felt his love grow. No, he didn't voice it, didn't say the words she wanted to hear, but he showed it in a thousand different, more important ways. And that was what mattered, she assured herself. The words would come when he was ready. In the meantime, she'd force herself to be patient, even if it killed her.

She had an appointment for Monday morning with her gynecologist. She wrote the time down on her personal calendar and then stuck it in the drawer of the phone table. It seemed, for once, that things were going right for her.

Annie called and they made plans for lunch and a day of hitting the malls. Shadow wanted to find something special for Brent for Christmas. She didn't know what it would be yet, but she'd come up with something.

She was deep in thought, contemplating shopping and loving Brent, when he came through the front door.

She went into his arms for a warm hug.

There was deep satisfaction in his eyes as he kissed her. Seconds later, he held out a small gift, beautifully wrapped in pink-and-silver foil. "I bought something for you."

Shadow stared at his hand, unblinking. "A Christmas present?"

"No. This is for now, today."

She still didn't take it. "Why?"

Brent barked a short laugh, took her hand and put the gift into it. "Because I wanted to give you something."

Her fingers curled around the small box, her hand shaking slightly. "You don't have to buy me things, Brent. I'm not Joan."

"I know you're nothing like Joan. You're not like any woman I've ever known." His voice grew soft. "I just saw this and wanted you to have it. Please. Open it."

Shadow carried the tiny package to the sofa and sat down, holding it in both hands. She gave Brent a tentative smile, then pulled loose the ribbon. She had a feeling she knew exactly what was in that small box and it made her insides quiver. She didn't want an extravagant piece of jewelry in place of Brent's love.

Gaudy diamonds or flashy chunks of gold meant less than nothing to her. She held her breath and lifted the lid.

Tears immediately sprang to her eyes. The ring was exquisite, simple and elegant and so unlike anything Shadow had ever seen before, she knew it was unique, just as Brent was. "Oh." The word emerged as two syllables, breathless and filled with wonder.

Two slender bands, one silver, one gold, twisted into a lover's knot, tied around a single perfect teardrop diamond. Brent saw the tears gathering in her eyes and asked hesitantly, "Do you like it? I know it's kind of different, but that's what I wanted for you. Something as special and one of a kind as you are."

Shadow held the ring in her fist and covered her face. She felt like a ninny, but tears overflowed her tightly closed eyes.

"You can have a different ring if you like." Brent sounded uncertain and unnerved by her show of emotion. "Hell, you can have anything you want. If you'd like a bigger diamond, a different setting, I'd be glad to take this back...."

He reached for the ring, but she snatched it to her chest. "Don't even think it!" Her bottom lip quivered as she looked at it again. "Oh, Brent. It's so beautiful."

After a silence, he said hesitantly, "You like it?"

"I *love* it." He stared hard at her, an intense expression in his eyes, and she added, "It's the most beautiful thing I've ever seen."

His smile was slow and hot. "To match the most beautiful woman I've ever seen."

"The cold has affected your brain." She continued admiring the ring.

Brent took her hand and slipped the ring from her

fingers. "I've asked you before. But you're the most stubborn woman I've ever known, so I'm asking you again. Shadow, will you marry me?"

She touched his face, loving him, and nodded. "Eventually."

"That's..." He stalled, her answer belatedly registering. His shoulders shook with silent laughter. "Always the unexpected, honey?"

"Always the truth."

Brent held her hand and carefully slid the ring over her finger. It was a perfect fit. He said, "I called your mother to ask what size to get."

"Oh, no! I'll never hear the end of it now! She'll be expecting us to get married soon."

Brent grinned wickedly. "I figured as much." He ducked as Shadow playfully swung at his head. "I'll take all the help I can get to convince you." He pulled her head down and whispered against her lips, "I want you."

The sudden lump in her throat wouldn't go away. She buried her face against his neck and held him tight. Would he ever tell her he loved her? Or were the words impossible for him to say?

Her heart ached; the ring felt warm and heavy on her hand. *Patience*, she reminded herself. But it was hard, so damned hard. She understood his reluctance; his only experiences with women had not been conducive to trust or sharing or true love. They were mercenary relationships, superficial and short-term. Brent was used to women who wanted something from him, not himself. It broke Shadow's heart to think of how he must have felt, knowing it was his bank account they found most attractive, not the man he was, not his character. It also left her feeling utterly helpless, because she could never again plan to marry without knowing there was love on both sides. She deserved that much. She wouldn't settle for less.

Shadow leaned forward, kissing him urgently, needing to show him her love, wanting him to see how important he was to her. She kissed his face, his nose, his eyes, his jaw. She heard his chuckle of appreciation. Her hands stroked over him, pushing clothes out of her way to feel his warm flesh, so hard and smooth, so strong.

Between returning her kisses, Brent made the enormous mistake of saying, "I should buy you jewelry more often. I love the way you show appreciation."

Shadow drew back. "Damn you, Brent Bramwell," she whispered, the words hoarse with emotion. She tried hard to tug the ring from her finger, but it was a snug fit and then Brent was there, covering her hands with his own.

"Hey, come on. I was only teasing."

"It's not funny," she tried to say, but the frustration was overwhelming, making it difficult to speak. "It's impossible for you, isn't it?" she finally asked. "You can't accept that I would love you, just *you*, for no other reason than that you're all I've ever wanted. And I'm not talking about money, damn you, so don't raise your eyebrow at me!"

"But that's a big part of me, Shadow. I am a businessman, a successful businessman. And even if I weren't, I come from money. I could have gone my entire life without ever working a job and not wanted for anything."

"You're wrong, Brent." She gave him a sad, deliberately pitying look. "You've been wanting all your life, only you won't admit it. At least I'm honest with myself. You could come back here tomorrow penniless and I wouldn't love you any less. Money never has and never will be one of my priorities."

Brent's laugh, filled with derision and disbelief, sounded forced to her discerning ears. "You would fall in love with a man who had no prospects, no way to support himself?"

"I didn't say that. You're not ignorant. I have no doubt you're more than capable of doing anything you put your mind to. You wouldn't starve or become helpless, waiting for others to do for you. That's not part of who you are, of your character. It's not a matter of finances, either. You're strong and self-confident, independent, intelligent, creative and compassionate—"

"Enough!" He rose to his feet, towering over her. "I'm not some damn paragon of humanity! I'm not perfect."

Shadow eyed him narrowly. "No. No, you're not. You're also insecure and cynical on occasion, and entirely too hung up on maintaining control. It's why you won't admit you love me, I think. If you do that, if you make that final commitment, I'd have a part of you, wouldn't I, Brent? I'd have some of the control. I could possibly use that against you, though exactly how escapes me since I love you and would never be able to bear seeing you hurt."

Brent turned away from her. He stalked the length of the front room a few times, and when he turned back to Shadow, she saw that he was in perfect control again, and she wanted to howl, to scream and rant and sit in the middle of the floor and cry like a baby. She did nothing, simply watching him, waiting.

"Look, sweetheart, this isn't what I intended when I gave you the ring. I thought you'd be happy about it. I want to marry you, I want to have children with you and live together and spend every available moment with you. I don't want to argue with you."

Shadow looked down at her hand. The beautiful ring caught a glimmer of light and reflected it, shining brilliantly. She wanted to take it off, to do the intelligent thing and save herself a lot of heartache. She wanted to hand it back to him and ask him to go.

But she couldn't. She shook her head, feeling more helpless than she could ever remember. She forced a small smile.

"I think I'll take a warm bath and go to bed early. I'm going shopping with a friend tomorrow. I'll be gone most of the day—that's how Annie and I shop. We do breakfast, then hit the stores, we do lunch and then hit the stores. When our legs get tired, we stop to have coffee and a doughnut or something. I haven't even started my Christmas shopping yet."

"Shadow..."

"There's some lunch meat in the fridge if you're hungry. And soup in the cabinet." She tried for another smile, but couldn't quite manage it. "I..." She shook her head, not sure there was anything else to say. She left the room in a hurry, unwilling to make him suffer through her tears. She was a coward and a fraud. She was a hypocrite of the worst sort. And she wanted so badly for Brent to love her she didn't think she could have stood there another single moment looking into his face, so filled as it was with uncertainty and confusion.

The warm bath did little to help her relax. She fought the tears, but they came anyway. She dunked her head under the water and scrubbed with a vengeance.

There were so many decisions to be made. If she was

pregnant, what would she do? Could she marry him with the very real possibility that he could never learn to trust her completely, never allow himself to love her as she wanted? Maybe she had been misreading him all along. Maybe this was as much as he had to give. He seemed to care for her, to actually love her, but if the words were never spoken, if he couldn't give voice to them, were they real? Would his love ever be the tangible, solid emotion she wanted?

She laid her cheek against her wet knees, drawn up in the tub. She supposed the bigger question, the only real issue, was could she give up on him? Could she let him go? And that answer was a resounding, emphatic *no*.

She wasn't a quitter. And Brent was far from a hopeless case.

With those thoughts in mind, she went about making herself as attractive as she knew how. She hadn't won Brent over by being herself, spontaneous and lighthearted. *Fun*. She would now try the calculated measures many women employed. She dabbed on perfume, brushed her hair until it shone, then slipped on the tiniest, sheerest teddy she owned.

It was a shimmering shade of creamy beige, nearly the same as her skin, giving her the appearance of nudity, but with decoration. The neckline scooped low, edged in a narrow rim of lace. Shadow surveyed herself in the mirror. She supposed she looked as attractive as possible. That Brent would appreciate the look, she didn't doubt. She slipped on a robe, then padded barefoot out of the bathroom.

BRENT PACED AROUND the kitchen pondering how things got so confused. Life used to be straightforward, easy to understand and easy to bend to his preferences. Until he'd met Shadow.

Damn, but she made him crazy. He'd already given her more of himself than any other woman he'd known. He'd asked her to marry him. But was that enough for her? No, she wanted more. She wanted things he wasn't certain he had to give.

He should just tell her he loved her. He'd told women that before; it was something expected during sex, and when he'd been younger, he'd also been more obliging. The words meant nothing.

But Shadow thought they did. And he believed her, believed that she felt that elusive swell of emotion that enabled her to commit herself completely to him. She felt and saw things other people never experienced, Brent included, which he supposed was one of the qualities he enjoyed most about her.

She was right about the control, too. He'd learned early in life that you had to command your own small portion of the world. Otherwise, people used you. It was human nature.

A dull ache started behind his eyes. He didn't know how to make things right with Shadow. He'd gladly give her anything, but he didn't know how to give her what she wanted. He couldn't lie to her and claim a feeling he wasn't certain of. She deserved better than that.

He leaned on the counter, staring out the kitchen window into the frozen darkness, and then he sensed her. His awareness of her was uncanny—one more thing he couldn't accept. Slowly he turned and there she stood, looking so beautiful she made him hard and hungry and needy.

He couldn't think of a single thing to say, so he

merely took in the sight of her, his soul somehow comforted by her presence even though his body went into spasms with her scent, her nearness. And that was another weakness, the way he felt more complete with her, which would indicate he was incomplete without her. *No.*

Her fingers toyed with the ends of the belt to her terry robe. Shoving away from the counter, Brent went to her, his hands hanging at his sides, his eyes watching her intently.

He wanted her. More than that, he craved her. Always. Very softly, he asked, "Ready for bed?"

She nodded.

Brent felt that damn lump stick in his throat again. He reached out to touch an impossibly soft curl above her left ear, twining it around his finger. "Did your bath make you feel better?"

Shadow took another step nearer him and he breathed in her scent, which was strangely different, like flowers, rather than herself. It was enticing and at the same time a bit unexpected. He liked her own scent. He wasn't used to her wearing perfume.

"I'm sorry, honey, for upsetting you. It was never my intent," he murmured. She lowered her head and her hair fell forward, hiding her face. He smoothed it back. She was so soft, so sweet. He raised his other hand, framing her face, his thumbs stroking over her temples. "I can't bear to see you cry, Shadow. I—"

"That was unforgivable," she said quickly, "and so unlike me. I hate tears. But I hate even more showing them to you. I'll try not to let that happen again."

Brent closed his eyes, pulling her close and pressing her cheek to his chest. Damn, she could rip him apart so easily. "Don't, sweetheart. Don't apologize to me and don't ever hide yourself, especially your upset, from me. I only meant I was sorry I caused you to cry, not that you shouldn't cry if you felt like it. Hell, everyone feels like it sometimes. Besides, you were entitled. I've been a jerk. You were right about getting a good night's sleep. You'll feel better in the morning."

Brent was so relieved to be able to sidestep Shadow's earlier accusations about love and commitment, he didn't at first notice her chagrined expression. When he did finally see that she was watching him with a touch of embarrassment and determination, he assumed it was caused by the awkwardness of their first real argument. Not wanting to, but seeing no way around it, he said, "Why don't you go on in to bed now. I'll be there in a bit."

She caught at his hand. "You can tuck me in and give me a good-night kiss, okay?"

Brent felt his heart kick into double time. He looked at Shadow's slender form as she led him toward the bedroom. Her bare toes peeked from beneath the edge of her robe. With each step, her hips swayed. The woman could incite his lust with nothing but a smile, and now her toes were turning him on.

Shadow stopped beside the bed and pulled back the spread. His stomach tightened, his thighs grew tense. Sometimes the wanting was so bad, so all encompassing, he thought he'd never get close enough to her, be with her enough, hold her enough.

Those times almost made him panic, which made him even more determined to retain control.

He was semihard by the time she finished preparing the bed. But as she turned, unknotting her belt and shrugging out of the robe, he gained full arousal, getting so hard he ached. Whatever she had planned, he was all for it.

"Damn," he whispered, spellbound by the sight of her in the revealing teddy. His gaze ran hungrily over her body, from the tips of her small pink toes to the vulnerable pulse in her exposed throat. He said again, very softly, *"Damn."*

Shadow reached out to unbutton his shirt. In a husky, enticing tone, she said, "If you won't give me your love, Brent, I'll have to take everything else that you've got."

Her fingertips touched his chest, tangled in his hair and then found his nipples. He shifted, but that didn't deter her. Her fingers drifted slowly down his abdomen, and lower still. "Sweetheart," he groaned, "whatever I have is yours."

She reached his belt and deftly unbuckled it. "I like your attitude, indeed I do. Just remember that sentiment," she warned softly, "because I fully intend to have it all."

It wasn't a threat that alarmed him. Not at all. In fact, at the moment...it thrilled the hell out of him.

10

BRENT WOKE EARLY the next morning, still slightly confused by the night's events. Shadow had been magnificent, giving and loving and quietly content. It was the quietly content part that alarmed him, because Shadow was not a quiet person. She was always bursting with energy and enthusiasm. Even in her sleep, she was so alive, so vibrant. But last night she'd been content. Damn.

He couldn't say exactly how she was different, only that he'd noticed the difference and didn't like it.

Was he the cause?

She'd taken their lovemaking too seriously. Shadow always found a dozen different reasons to laugh and tease and smile whenever they made love, but last night had been almost grave. And her gravity, having replaced her unique form of fun, had Brent scowling, even though Shadow was cuddled against him, her body soft and warm.

He lay silently in the dark, holding her close, trying to decipher in his mind what had gone wrong and how he could fix it. Shadow was trying to change on him and that thought was enough to give him cramps. Damn it, he wanted her just the way she was.

She wanted his love—she'd said as much in her bold, blatant way—but did she think changing herself was a means to an end? He wouldn't have it.

Driven by his tumultuous thoughts, Brent glanced at the clock. It was only six o'clock. He slipped into the bathroom to shower. Half an hour later, he was dressed and sipping coffee in the kitchen. He wanted to relax, but couldn't. He was a coward, which was an entirely new concept for him. He couldn't recall ever fearing anybody or anything. But Shadow scared the hell out of him, just as he'd once told her. However, this time his fear was motivated more from the very real possibility of losing her than from her lack of caution.

If he didn't give her the love she wanted, would she leave him? That asinine thought made him laugh with self-mockery. Who was he kidding? Not himself, surely, because he knew that without her, he'd be miserable. Though he'd fought it hard, if he was honest, if he looked inside himself, he'd admit that she had his love. Hell, she'd owned it almost from the first moment he'd seen her and summarily fallen on his ass.

Brent finished his coffee with a gulp. Being a decisive man by nature, he made up his mind in a heartbeat. He'd never quailed from the truth before and damned if he'd start now. He wanted to pull her from her bed, to wake her with kisses and touches and the words she'd almost demanded to hear.

He wanted her laughing again, teasing him even as she drove him over the edge.

But he wasn't a selfish man. He'd kept her up most of the night and she needed her sleep.

Brent decided to leave her a note, to tell her to plan on going out for dinner, someplace nice. Maybe she would wear black for him again. The thought made him chuckle.

He went to the small telephone table to hunt up a

pencil and paper. And it was then, rummaging through the drawer, that he found her calendar with the appointment for the gynecologist written in on Monday.

SHADOW WOKE WITH A START when the bedroom door opened. Brent stood in the doorway.

He flipped on the light, temporarily blinding her, and when she managed to open her left eye a crack, she saw he was angry.

"What's the matter?"

"Why didn't you tell me? And don't try to claim this is your regular checkup. You think you're pregnant, don't you?"

Shadow blinked, rubbing her face tiredly. Through her fingers she saw that Brent had her calendar in his right hand. Then she peeked up at his face. *Oh boy*.

"I suppose," she said around a yawn, "it's a possibility, since I didn't start my period on time. I thought I'd have it confirmed before I said anything."

Brent sat on the side of the bed. "You would have told me, one way or the other? You're certain?"

She couldn't lie to Brent, but sometimes innate honesty was a real pain in the butt. "Probably."

He exploded. "What the hell does that mean? Probably? Would you have told me or not if you'd found out you were pregnant?"

Shadow closed her eyes a moment. "I most likely would have told you right away. I'm not really dishonest, and I know you would want to be a part of your baby's life. But I kept thinking... Brent, do you realize how hard it would be on me? Seeing you constantly, having you nearby, if we weren't still intimate, if we weren't a couple?'' She looked away, suffused with guilt. "I just don't know if I could bear that."

Brent went very still. His eyes narrowed and a nerve ticked in his jaw. "Were you planning on calling it quits?" he asked in a deadly calm voice. "Is that what this is all about?"

"No." She shook her head adamantly. "I decided last night I couldn't give up on you. But I don't know if I can be what you want, Brent, if I can be someone you can love."

His angry expression crumpled, and his eyes filled with pain. Shadow rushed on. "Love is necessary, Brent. Especially if we're going to raise a baby together. I could maybe get by without ever having you love me. I'm tough, you know," she said, trying for a spot of humor. "But a baby, well, that's different."

He stood and she grabbed his hand. "Please, Brent. Try to understand—"

"Oh, I understand. Perfectly." He walked to the window and stood there looking out. Shadow couldn't see anything of interest beyond a very fat moon hovering low in the darkened sky. Finally he said, "I think it's past time we talked. Seriously."

Scooting up in the bed, Shadow wrapped her arms tight around her bent knees and bit down hard on her bottom lip, refusing to cry again.

Brent turned to her, giving her a small strained smile. "I was going to suggest we go out for dinner tonight. With the weather so disagreeable, we haven't been out much lately. What do you think?"

Shadow stared at the blanket covering her feet. Dinner? He wanted to go for dinner? She looked up at him, drowning in confusion. "But I thought—"

"Shh. We'll talk tonight." He came to her, leaning

over the bed and trapping her between his out-
stretched arms, his hands braced on the headboard. "I
think we both need a little time to think, don't you?"

Not really, but she nodded anyway. Brent gave her
another small, tight smile, then touched his mouth to
hers, so very gently her eyes filled with tears despite
her resolve.

"Have fun shopping and remember to—"

"Be careful," she finished for him. "I will." She
waited, but he didn't say anything else. He left the
room silently and a moment later she heard the front
door close.

With a deep sigh, Shadow forced herself from the
bed. She was an optimist, she reminded herself. Everything would work out for the best.

But as she dressed and prepared to leave to meet
with Annie, her mind drifted back to Brent. He'd been
awfully quiet, introspective. She wished she could read
his thoughts, know what, exactly, he felt. He had been
angry, she wasn't wrong about that. But he'd also
looked sad. Right before he left, he'd seemed very determined. She shook her head in wonder.

It was a good thing she'd planned on shopping because she definitely needed a distraction. Her last
thought as she walked out the door was that even another disturbance from her so-called admirer would almost be welcome. Anything to keep her mind off Brent
and the fiasco she'd made of their relationship.

THERE'S A WISE SAYING that claims you should be careful what you wish for, or you just might get it. Shadow
would later wonder if she should have that sentiment
embroidered and hung on her wall.

She was already in her car when she realized she'd

forgotten her shopping list. Feeling like a dunce, she walked back to the house. But the moment she reached the front door, she felt someone looking at her.

She turned, and came face-to-face with Chad Moreland. He stood uncertainly on the bottom step of the porch.

She stared, a little stunned, a little confused and plenty alarmed.

Red swollen eyes glared at her and he said in a voice hoarse and deep, "I saw you leave," then immediately broke into a fit of coughing. His body was racked with it, the sound pitiful and strained.

Shadow blinked at him, watching as he grabbed the handrail for support. As if in pain, he bent low while more coughs shook his body.

She saw quite a bit in that moment. The handsome man who'd entered her contest no longer existed. This young man looked ravaged. He was dirty, badly in need of a shower, his clothes wrinkled and worn. A scraggly smattering of beard stubble covered his gaunt cheeks and his face was pale, sallow. He was sick, very sick, she realized, and wondered what to do.

When his coughing subsided, he held his chest and stared at her.

"I...I came back for my list." Shadow watched him closely, scared, but even more concerned. "Chad, what's wrong with you? What are you doing here?"

He laughed, the sound raw and ugly. He started up the steps toward her, but stumbled drunkenly. He stopped and held the railing again, scowling at her. "He doesn't deserve you! You're wasting yourself on him and you've made me so angry, Shadow. Very angry."

She suffered a stunned silence.

Chad hitched a dirty finger over his shoulder. "Let's go in the house where it's warm. I want to talk to you."

She shook her head. "I don't think so."

"Don't be afraid," he cajoled, his voice now low and wheezing. "I'd never hurt you. We just need to figure out how to get rid of him."

Her heart shot into her throat and she said without thinking, "You stay away from Brent!"

He scowled darkly, stepped toward her. "You can't want him," he rasped. "You can't—" The words splintered, interrupted by another round of hacking, breath-stealing coughs. He crumpled to his knees, a fist squeezed to his chest.

Shadow made an instinctive move toward him, but halted. What to do? She'd never seen a man so pitifully weak and ill, but he was still dangerous, unpredictable.

He broke into her thoughts, his words now slurred with fatigue. "I put something on your cookies...something to make you pass out so you wouldn't sleep with him. You were so nice to me...."

Sudden anger overshadowed her fear. *"You poisoned my cookies?"*

He smirked. "I was going to come over and take care of you. But he stayed." He maneuvered another step closer. "Why him, Shadow? Why do you want him?"

Chad was a pharmacist, she remembered with dawning horror. He'd used his knowledge of drugs against her. "How did you get to my cookies?" The thought that he might have been in her house made her ill all over again.

"You left the bag in your car. You always park so far out, it was easy to sprinkle something on them. Everyone knows you never lock your car."

He drew himself up, weaving on his feet, and gained

yet another step. He was closer now, too close, and she pressed herself backward even as she heard him say, "I didn't want you with him, but he stayed, even though I knew you were sleeping. He stayed and you let him!"

She backed up, explaining stupidly, while stalling for time, "It's this seven-year-itch thing, I think. It's just my time—"

He took the final step, a low growl emerging.

Shadow didn't delude herself into thinking she was a physical match for him, even in his weakened condition. She wondered if she could make it into the house, to the phone. Chad read her intent and lurched forward, wanting to reach her.

But he was too weak. He hit a patch of ice, flailed about, then stumbled off the top step. His legs buckled beneath him and he screamed. As Shadow watched in horror, he tumbled, his body limp, crashing several times into the railing before landing with a sickening thud at the bottom of the porch steps. His head cracked hard against the icy walkway and a small patch of blood appeared.

He moaned softly, galvanizing Shadow into action. Rushing toward him, she cried, "Chad? Are you all right?"

He grabbed her hand, his grip surprisingly strong, his flesh burning with fever. "I'm so damn cold," he whimpered. His eyes rolled into his head and he quieted, his body going still.

BRENT WAS MORE THAN a little distracted when his secretary buzzed him. "Yeah, Micky, what is it?"

"You have a personal call on line two."

Brent tensed, a typical reaction for him. Wherever Shadow was concerned he suffered from extremes, both sexual and emotional. "I'll take it. Thanks, Micky."

Releasing the intercom button, Brent hesitated. He'd been thinking about her all morning, wanting to call her, wishing he'd admitted his love this morning rather than putting it off. He'd been ridiculous and he knew it. Shadow felt hurt over his attitude, thinking him ambivalent to her. It pained him every time he remembered the look on her face, her admission that it would be too much to see him regularly, knowing he didn't love her.

It was past time to set things right with her. He picked up the receiver and settled back in his chair. "Hello, sweetheart. Done with your shopping so soon?"

"Uh, I hope the sweetheart you're referring to is Shadow. But I'm not her. I'm her friend Annie."

Brent went still. "I'm sorry, I just assumed...is anything wrong? Where's Shadow?"

"That's just it. I have no idea. I was afraid something was wrong because she's never stood me up before."

"Stood you up?" He shot forward in his seat again. "What the hell do you mean? Where is she?"

"I already told you, I don't know. She was supposed to meet me at the mall. I waited and waited, but she didn't show and now I'm worried."

"She never called?"

"No. I tried phoning her house, but there was no answer. She gave me your name and number awhile back, so...I tried you." There was a heavy pause, filled with worry. "You really don't know where she is?"

"Go back to your place in case she tries to call you. I'm going home to check there right now."

As if his urgency alarmed her even more, Annie said

hurriedly, "Please, let me know if you find her! She told me about that guy who's been calling—"

"Yeah." Brent cursed low, then forced himself to be calm. Trying to convince himself as much as Annie, he said, "I'm sure everything's okay. Don't worry. I'll find her."

He hung up and was out of his seat in the same movement. As he passed his secretary, he said, "If Ms. Callahan calls, let me know immediately. I'll be at home." He started out, then thought to clarify, "Not my house, but—"

"Yes, sir. I know."

"Thanks, Micky."

Brent made it home in record time. His heart pounded heavily, his teeth were clenched in fear. If anything happened to her... He couldn't, wouldn't finish that thought. His palms were sweaty by the time he pulled into the driveway.

He ran up the walkway, then came to a staggering halt. "Oh, God, no." A patch of dark blood made a stark contrast to the white snow at the bottom of the steps. He stared at it, his insides twisting, his heart knocking in his chest. In that moment, he suffered a fear he'd never known before, a blackness that obliterated every other sensation. He couldn't breathe, couldn't think.

It hit him—a desperate hope that she might have merely hurt herself, then gone inside.

Praying, he went up the steps in one jump, jerked the door open and shouted her name. No answer. He went through the house at a dead run, again calling out for her. He stopped, not knowing what to do.

He squeezed his eyes shut, then jerked around when

the phone gave a shrill ring. He grabbed it up, his voice gruff with emotion. "Shadow?"

"It's Micky, Mr. Bramwell. I—"

"Where is she, Micky?" The words were choked, raw.

Very gently, Micky said, "She's fine, sir. She just called. She's at Memorial Hospital—"

Brent dropped the phone. Memorial was only a short drive away, but at the moment, it seemed like the span of a continent. All his good intentions, the alarm system, his constant reminders for caution—they hadn't been enough. *He* hadn't done enough.

He drove like a madman, alternating between silent threats and thoughts of retribution, to heartfelt prayers that she'd be all right, that she would eventually forgive him his stupidity.

She was a part of him, the most important part. The part that made him smile and filled him with happiness and security.

He loved her. And there was a very good chance he'd waited too long to tell her.

SHADOW PACED THE HALLWAY, exhausted from all the questions the police had asked her. She wished Brent would come, just to hold her hand if nothing else.

She didn't know if Chad was going to live. He'd seemed so sick, and the doctor had come out to tell her he had a bad case of pneumonia and a concussion. He'd spent so much time outside, spying on her, rather than seeking a doctor when he became ill. He'd gone into a coma shortly after Shadow had gotten him to the hospital, and he hadn't opened his eyes since. His condition was critical. Shadow, unbelievably, felt responsible for him. She couldn't leave without first finding out if he'd be okay.

But she would have appreciated Brent's support. She had, after all, been through a lot. It wasn't every day that you had a near delirious madman bleeding all over your car, reciting in great, babbling detail all the ways he loved you.

The irony of it had nearly choked her. She had an unwelcome and unhealthy declaration from Chad, yet Brent, the man she loved, wouldn't even hint at such words.

Damn, she wished Brent were here now.

As if summoned by her, he burst through the waiting room doors at that precise moment. He looked like a wild man, and Shadow automatically groped behind her for the nearest chair.

Brent saw her, and his expression shattered. His chest heaved and then, with a fast, purposeful stride, he started toward her.

No sooner did he take a step in her direction than two men standing nearby—one an orderly, by the looks of him, the other a guard—tried to stop him. Brent shrugged off their restraining hands, his gaze never leaving Shadow. He was gripped more firmly and promptly shoved against the wall.

Shadow's eyes widened. In a rush, she explained, "He's with me. He...he must have been worried?" It sounded like a question—it *was* a question! Whatever was the matter with him?

Brent reached her, then literally hauled her off her feet and into his arms. "Are you hurt?"

"No," she squeaked, still unsure of his mood.

He reared back, gently shaking her. "You're all right? You swear?"

"I'm fine."

All the rigidity left his body with one deep breath.

He hugged her to him, treating her to a bone-crushing embrace, her feet still dangling off the floor. "God, you scared me," he mumbled into her neck, and Shadow could feel him trembling.

She stroked his back. "Brent, I'm fine. Didn't your secretary give you my message?"

He shook his head, unwilling to release her just to explain. He hadn't given Micky the chance to speak, he had been so overwhelmed with terror.

Aware of the curious glances from the other occupants of the waiting room, Shadow whispered, "Brent, put me down now. It's okay."

He lowered her into her seat, but he didn't release her, which meant he ended up kneeling in front of her, his head still buried against her neck.

Shadow became worried. "Brent?"

"I love you, sweetheart. God, I love you so damned much it's killing me."

Stunned, Shadow took a moment to digest that bit of information, and then she grinned an enormous grin. "Well, for heaven's sake, don't die!" she exclaimed, then added more softly, "Just keep on loving me. Always."

Brent squeezed her closer. Shadow had to protest or end up in a faint because she positively couldn't breathe. At her first grunt, Brent loosened his arms, then leaned back, but not too far back. His hands came up to frame her face and he said again, "I love you. If you love me, too, even a little, you won't ever scare me like that again. Promise me."

Her eyes filled with tears and this time she didn't mind in the least. "I promise."

"Good." He stood suddenly, his hands fisted on his hips. "Where the hell is he?"

And Shadow saw the murderous intent in his eyes.

"He has pneumonia, and on top of that, he fell down the steps and gave himself a concussion. Right this minute, he isn't even conscious!"

Brent closed his eyes. "That was his blood, then, that I saw at the bottom of the steps?"

"Yes. You didn't think... Oh, Brent. I'm sorry."

"It doesn't matter now." Then he looked at her in disbelief. "Don't tell me you're feeling sorry for him!"

"In a way I am. He's so pitiful."

Brent clenched his jaw, a telling sign that he wasn't as forgiving.

"He put something on my cookies," she admitted. "That's why I fell asleep so suddenly. He wanted to keep us from making love. He's so sick, Brent. I mean, mentally. He needs help."

"I'll kill the bastard."

A young officer approached, the same one who had asked Shadow dozens of questions earlier. She gave him a wan smile, then introduced him to Brent.

Officer Grange nodded. "The doctor just spoke with me. They have him stabilized, but he hasn't regained consciousness. There's no need for you to stay. We'll need to know where to reach you, however."

Brent gave him his own address. "We'll be getting married, soon. Anytime you need her, try my number."

That got a smile from both Shadow and Officer Grange.

"I'm really sorry for what you've been through," Grange offered. "At least he got caught before either of you were hurt. You shouldn't have any more trouble from him. There are other officers at the house right now, looking over the scene, taking evidence. You can rest easy now."

Brent shook his head. "You must not know Ms. Callahan very well. You can never rest easy around her. You have to keep on your toes...or she'll stomp all over them."

Shadow punched playfully at Brent's shoulder. Then allowed him, with a small show of resistance, to lead her from the hospital. Despite everything that had happened, she felt good. Very, very good.

THE MORNING SUNSHINE WAS bright as Brent stretched awake. The snow was gone, and the May weather had turned mild. He smoothed his hand over Shadow's hip and rumbled, "G'morning, sweetheart."

"Hmm," she whispered back, wiggling her hips into his lap.

Brent's hand went to her belly and he asked, "Any morning sickness?"

"No. I guess the doctor was right," she said around a yawn and an elaborate stretch. "The second trimester isn't so bad."

"I'm glad the first was a false alarm. Your parents will like it better that the baby's born nine months after the wedding and not a day before."

"Maybe. But they would have been thrilled either way."

"I know. My mom was ecstatic over the idea of a grandchild. She was a little concerned, though, over what you might name the future Bramwell."

Grinning wickedly, Shadow said, "I told her I favored mythology over weather conditions. How do you like Zeus? Or Aphrodite?"

Brent bent to kiss her shoulder. "I love you, Shadow."

"You've gotten so good at saying that."

"Well, you see, this slightly goofy, unbelievably sexy woman I know insisted on showing me how much fun love can be."

"She convinced you, did she?"

"Yes, she surely did. And she'll be stuck with me now. Forever."

"Hey, she sounds like one lucky broad to me."

*Three sizzling love stories
by today's hottest writers
can be found in...*

Midnight Fantasies....

Feel the heat!

Available June 2001

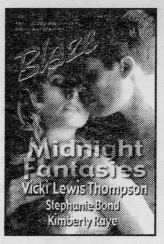

MYSTERY LOVER—*Vicki Lewis Thompson*
When an unexpected storm hits, rancher Jonas Garfield
takes cover in a nearby cave...and finds himself seduced
senseless by an enigmatic temptress who refuses to tell him
her name. All he knows is that this sexy woman wants him.
And for Jonas, that's enough—for now....

AFTER HOURS—*Stephanie Bond*
Michael Pierce has always considered costume shop
owner Rebecca Valentine no more than an associate—
until he drops by her shop one night and witnesses the
mousy wallflower's transformation into a seductive siren.
Suddenly he's desperate to know her much better.
But which woman is the real Rebecca?

SHOW AND TELL—*Kimberly Raye*
A naughty lingerie party. A forbidden fantasy. When Texas
bad boy Dallas Jericho finds a slip of paper left over from
the party, he is surprised—and aroused—to discover that he
is good girl Laney Merriweather's wildest fantasy. So what
can he do but show the lady what she's been missing....

Visit us at www.eHarlequin.com   PHMIDNIGHT

Meet 50 loving dads in

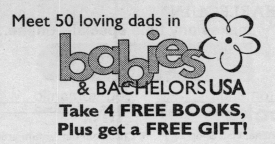

& BACHELORS USA
Take 4 FREE BOOKS,
Plus get a FREE GIFT!

Babies & Bachelors USA is a heartwarming new collection of reissued novels featuring 50 sexy heroes from every state who experience the ups and downs of fatherhood and find time for love all the same. All of the books, hand-picked by our editors, are outstanding romances by some of the world's bestselling authors, including Stella Bagwell, Kristine Rolofson, Judith Arnold and Marie Ferrarella!

Don't delay, order today! Call customer service at
1-800-873-8635.
Or
Clip this page and mail to The Reader Service:

In U.S.A.
P.O. Box 9049
Buffalo, NY
14269-9049

In CANADA
P.O. Box 616
Fort Erie, Ontario
L2A 5X3

YES! Please send me four FREE BOOKS and FREE GIFT along with the next four novels on a 14-day free home preview. If I like the books and decide to keep them, I'll pay just $15.96* U.S. or $18.00* CAN., and there's no charge for shipping and handling. Otherwise, I'll keep the 4 FREE BOOKS and FREE GIFT and return the rest. If I decide to continue, I'll receive six books each month—two of which are always free—until I've received the entire collection. In other words, if I collect all 50 volumes, I will have paid for 32 and received 18 absolutely free!

267 HCK 4537
467 HCK 4538

Name	(Please Print)		
Address			Apt. #
City		State/Prov.	Zip/Postal Code

* Terms and prices subject to change without notice.
  Sales Tax applicable in N.Y. Canadian residents will be charged applicable provincial taxes and GST. All orders are subject to approval.

DIRBAB02

© 2000 Harlequin Enterprises Limited

HARLEQUIN®

makes any time special—online...

eHARLEQUIN.com

your romantic
books

♥ **Shop online! Visit Shop eHarlequin and discover a wide selection of new releases and classic favorites at great discounted prices.**

♥ **Read our daily and weekly Internet exclusive serials, and participate in our interactive novel in the reading room.**

♥ **Ever dreamed of being a writer? Enter your chapter for a chance to become a featured author in our Writing Round Robin novel.**

your romantic
life

♥ **Check out our feature articles on dating, flirting and other important romance topics and get your daily love dose with tips on how to keep the romance alive every day.**

• • • • • •

your
community

♥ **Have a Heart-to-Heart with other members about the latest books and meet your favorite authors.**

♥ **Discuss your romantic dilemma in the Tales from the Heart message board.**

your romantic
escapes

♥ **Learn what the stars have in store for you with our daily Passionscopes and weekly Erotiscopes.**

♥ **Get the latest scoop on your favorite royals in Royal Romance.**

**All this and more available at
www.eHarlequin.com
on Women.com Networks**

HINTA1R

*Harlequin truly does
make any time special....
This year we are celebrating
weddings in style!*

A Walk Down the Aisle
WEDDING CELEBRATION

To help us celebrate, we want you to tell us how wearing the Harlequin wedding gown will make your wedding day special. As the grand prize, Harlequin will offer one lucky bride the chance to **"Walk Down the Aisle" in the Harlequin wedding gown!**

There's more...

For her honeymoon, she and her groom will spend five nights at the **Hyatt Regency Maui.** As part of this five-night honeymoon at the hotel renowned for its romantic attractions, the couple will enjoy a candlelit dinner for two in Swan Court, a sunset sail on the hotel's catamaran, and duet spa treatments.

A HYATT RESORT AND SPA®

Maui • Molokai • Lanai

To enter, please write, in, 250 words or less, how wearing the Harlequin wedding gown will make your wedding day special. The entry will be judged based on its emotionally compelling nature, its originality and creativity, and its sincerity. This contest is open to Canadian and U.S. residents only and to those who are 18 years of age and older. There is no purchase necessary to enter. Void where prohibited. See further contest rules attached. Please send your entry to:

Walk Down the Aisle Contest

In Canada
P.O. Box 637
Fort Erie, Ontario
L2A 5X3

In U.S.A.
P.O. Box 9076
3010 Walden Ave.
Buffalo, NY 14269-9076

You can also enter by visiting www.eHarlequin.com
Win the Harlequin wedding gown and the vacation of a lifetime!
The deadline for entries is October 1, 2001.

HARLEQUIN®
Makes any time special ®

PHWDACONT1

HARLEQUIN WALK DOWN THE AISLE TO MAUI CONTEST 1197
OFFICIAL RULES
NO PURCHASE NECESSARY TO ENTER

1. To enter, follow directions published in the offer to which you are responding. Contest begins April 2, 2001, and ends on October 1, 2001. Method of entry may vary. Mailed entries must be postmarked by October 1, 2001, and received by October 8, 2001.

2. Contest entry may be, at times, presented via the Internet, but will be restricted solely to residents of certain geographic areas that are disclosed on the Web site. To enter via the Internet, if permissible, access the Harlequin Web site (www.eHarlequin.com) and follow the directions displayed online. Online entries must be received by 11:59 p.m. E.S.T. on October 1, 2001.

   In lieu of submitting an entry online, enter by mail by hand-printing (or typing) on an 8½" x 11" plain piece of paper, your name, address (including zip code), Contest number/name and in 250 words or fewer, why winning a Harlequin wedding dress would make your wedding day special. Mail via first-class mail to: Harlequin Walk Down the Aisle Contest 1197, (in the U.S.) P.O. Box 9076, 3010 Walden Avenue, Buffalo, NY 14269-9076, (in Canada) P.O. Box 637, Fort Erie, Ontario L2A 5X3, Canada. Limit one entry per person, household address and e-mail address. Online and/or mailed entries received from persons residing in geographic areas in which Internet entry is not permissible will be disqualified.

3. Contests will be judged by a panel of members of the Harlequin editorial, marketing and public relations staff based on the following criteria:

   • Originality and Creativity—50%
   • Emotionally Compelling—25%
   • Sincerity—25%

   In the event of a tie, duplicate prizes will be awarded. Decisions of the judges are final.

4. All entries become the property of Torstar Corp. and will not be returned. No responsibility is assumed for lost, late, illegible, incomplete, inaccurate, nondelivered or misdirected mail or misdirected e-mail, for technical, hardware or software failures of any kind, lost or unavailable network connections, or failed, incomplete, garbled or delayed computer transmission or any human error which may occur in the receipt or processing of the entries in this Contest.

5. Contest open only to residents of the U.S. (except Puerto Rico) and Canada, who are 18 years of age or older, and is void wherever prohibited by law; all applicable laws and regulations apply. Any litigation within the Province of Quebec respecting the conduct or organization of a publicity contest may be submitted to the Régie des alcools, des courses et des jeux for a ruling. Any litigation respecting the awarding of a prize may be submitted to the Régie des alcools, des courses et des jeux only for the purpose of helping the parties reach a settlement. Employees and immediate family members of Torstar Corp. and D. L. Blair, Inc., their affiliates, subsidiaries and all other agencies, entities and persons connected with the use, marketing or conduct of this Contest are not eligible to enter. Taxes on prizes are the sole responsibility of winners. Acceptance of any prize offered constitutes permission to use winner's name, photograph or other likeness for the purposes of advertising, trade and promotion on behalf of Torstar Corp., its affiliates and subsidiaries without further compensation to the winner, unless prohibited by law.

6. Winners will be determined no later than November 15, 2001, and will be notified by mail. Winners will be required to sign and return an Affidavit of Eligibility form within 15 days after winner notification. Noncompliance within that time period may result in disqualification and an alternative winner may be selected. Winners of trip must execute a Release of Liability prior to ticketing and must possess required travel documents (e.g. passport, photo ID) where applicable. Trip must be completed by November 2002. No substitution of prize permitted by winner. Torstar Corp. and D. L. Blair, Inc., their parents, affiliates, and subsidiaries are not responsible for errors in printing or electronic presentation of Contest, entries and/or game pieces. In the event of printing or other errors which may result in unintended prize values or duplication of prizes, all affected game pieces or entries shall be null and void. If for any reason the Internet portion of the Contest is not capable of running as planned, including infection by computer virus, bugs, tampering, unauthorized intervention, fraud, technical failures, or any other causes beyond the control of Torstar Corp. which corrupt or affect the administration, secrecy, fairness, integrity or proper conduct of the Contest, Torstar Corp. reserves the right, at its sole discretion, to disqualify any individual who tampers with the entry process and to cancel, terminate, modify or suspend the Contest or the Internet portion thereof. In the event of a dispute regarding an online entry, the entry will be deemed submitted by the authorized holder of the e-mail account submitted at the time of entry. Authorized account holder is defined as the natural person who is assigned to an e-mail address by an Internet access provider, online service provider or other organization that is responsible for arranging e-mail address for the domain associated with the submitted e-mail address. **Purchase or acceptance of a product offer does not improve your chances of winning.**

7. Prizes: (1) Grand Prize—A Harlequin wedding dress (approximate retail value: $3,500) and a 5-night/6-day honeymoon trip to Maui, HI, including round-trip air transportation provided by Maui Visitors Bureau from Los Angeles International Airport (winner is responsible for transportation to and from Los Angeles International Airport) and a Harlequin Romance Package, including hotel accomodations (double occupancy) at the Hyatt Regency Maui Resort and Spa, dinner for (2) two at Swan Court, a sunset sail on Kiele V and a spa treatment for the winner (approximate retail value: $4,000); (5) Five runner-up prizes of a $1000 gift certificate to selected retail outlets to be determined by Sponsor (retail value $1000 ea.). Prizes consist of only those items listed as part of the prize. Limit one prize per person. All prizes are valued in U.S. currency.

8. For a list of winners (available after December 17, 2001) send a self-addressed, stamped envelope to: Harlequin Walk Down the Aisle Contest 1197 Winners, P.O. Box 4200 Blair, NE 68009-4200 or you may access the www.eHarlequin.com Web site through January 15, 2002.

Contest sponsored by Torstar Corp., P.O. Box 9042, Buffalo, NY 14269-9042, U.S.A.

PHWDACONT2